RESCUED IN A
WEDDING DRESS

RESCUED IN A
WEDDING DRESS

BY

CARA COLTER

First published in Great Britain 2010
Large Print edition 2011
Harlequin Mills & Boon Limited,
Eton House, 18-24 Paradise Road,
Richmond, Surrey TW9 1SR

© Cara Colter 2010

ISBN: 978 0 263 21570 0

Harlequin Mills & Boon policy is to use papers that are
natural, renewable and recyclable products and made
from wood grown in sustainable forests. The logging and
manufacturing process conform to the legal environmental
regulations of the country of origin.

Printed and bound in Great Britain
by CPI Antony Rowe, Chippenham, Wiltshire

CHAPTER ONE

MOLLY MICHAELS stared at the contents of the large rectangular box that had been set haphazardly on top of the clutter on her desk. The box contained a wedding gown.

Over the weekend donations that were intended for one of the three New York City secondhand clothing shops that were owned and operated by Second Chances Charity Inc—and that provided the funding for their community programs—often ended up here, stacked outside the doorstep of their main office.

It did seem like a cruel irony, though, that this donation would end up on *her* desk.

"Sworn off love," Molly told herself, firmly, and shut the box. "Allergic to amour. Lessons learned. Doors closed."

She turned and hung up her coat in the closet of her tiny office, then returned to her desk. She snuck the box lid open, just a crack, then opened it just a little more. The dress was a confection. It looked like it had been spun out of dreams and silk.

"Pained by passion," Molly reminded herself, but even as she did, her hand stole into the box, and her fingers touched the delicate delight of the gloriously rich fabric.

What would it hurt to *look?* It could even be a good exercise for her. Her relationship with Chuck, her broken engagement, was six months in the past. The dress was probably ridiculous. Looking at it, and feeling *nothing,* better yet *judging* it, would be a good test of the new her.

Molly Michaels was one hundred percent career woman now, absolutely dedicated to her work here as the project manager at Second Chances. It was her job to select, implement and maintain the programs the charity funded that helped people in some of New York's most challenged neighborhoods.

"Love my career. Totally satisfied," she muttered. "Completely fulfilled!"

She slipped the pure white dress out of the box, felt the sensuous slide of the fabric across her palms as she shook it out.

The dress *was* ridiculous. And the total embodiment of romance. Ethereal as a puff of smoke, soft as a whisper, the layers and layers of ruffles glittered with hundreds of hand-sewn pearls and tiny silk flowers. The designer label attested to the fact that someone had spent a fortune on it.

And the fact it had shown up here was a reminder that all those romantic dreams had a treacherous tendency to go sideways. Who sent their dress, their most poignant reminder of their special day, to a charity that specialized in secondhand sales, if things had gone well?

So, it wasn't just *her* who had been burned by love. *Au contraire!* It was the way of the world.

Still, despite her efforts to talk sense to herself, there was no denying the little twist of wistfulness in her tummy as Molly looked at the dress, *felt* all a dress like that could stand for. *Love.*

Souls joined. Laughter shared. Long conversations. Lonely no more.

Molly was disappointed in herself for entertaining the hopelessly naive thoughts, even briefly. She wanted to kill that renegade longing that stirred in her. The logical way to do that would be to put the dress back in the box, and have the receptionist, Tish, send it off to the best of Second Chances stores, Wow and Then, on the Upper West Side. That store specialized in high-end gently used fashions. Everything with a designer label in it ended up there.

But, sadly, Molly had never been logical. Sadly, she had not missed the fact the dress was *exactly* her size.

On impulse, she decided the best way to face her shattered dreams head-on would be to put on the dress. She would face the bride she was never going to be in the mirror. She would regain her power over those ever so foolish and hopelessly old-fashioned dreams of *ever after.*

How could she, of all people, believe such nonsense? Why was it that the constant squabbling of her parents, the eventual dissolution of her family, her mother remarrying *often,* had not prepared Molly for real life? No, rather than making her put aside her belief in love, her dreams of a family, her disappointment-filled childhood had instead made her *yearn* for those things.

That yearning had been drastic enough to make her ignore every warning sign Chuck had given her. And there had been plenty of them! Not at first, of course. At first, it had been all delight and devotion. But then, Molly had caught her intended in increasingly frequent insults: little white lies, lateness, dates not kept.

She had forgiven him, allowing herself to believe that a loving heart overlooked the small slights, the inconsiderations, the occasional surliness, the lack of enthusiasm for the things she liked to do. She had managed to minimize the fact that the engagement ring had been embarrassingly tiny, and efforts to address setting a date had been rebuffed.

In other words, Molly had been so engrossed in her fantasy about love, had been so focused on a day and a dress just like this one, that she had excused and tolerated and dismissed behavior that, in retrospect, had been humiliatingly unacceptable.

Now she was anxious to prove to herself that a dress like this one had no power over her at all. None! Her days of being a hopeless dreamer, of being naive, of being romantic to the point of being pathetic, were over.

Over and done. Molly Michaels was a new woman, one who could put on a dress like this and *scoff* at the beliefs it represented. *Round-faced babies, a bassinet beside the bed, seaside holidays, chasing children through the sand, cuddling around a roaring fire with him, the dream man, beside you singing songs and toasting marshmallows.*

"Dream man is right," she scolded herself. "Because that's where such a man exists. In dreams."

The dress proved harder to get on than Molly could have imagined, which should have made her give it up. Instead, it made her more determined, which formed an unfortunate parallel to her past relationship.

The harder it had been with Chuck, the more she had tried to make it work.

That desperate-for-love woman was being left behind her, and putting on this dress was going to be one more step in helping her do it!

But first she got tangled in the sewn-in lining, and spent a few helpless moments lost in the voluminous sea of white fabric. When her head finally popped out the correct opening, her hair was caught hard in one of the pearls that encrusted the neckline. After she had got free of that, fate made one more last-ditch effort to get her to stop this nonsense. The back of the dress was not designed to be done up single-handedly.

Still, having come this far, with much determination and contortion, Molly somehow managed to get every single fastener closed, though it felt as if she had pulled the muscle in her left shoulder in the process.

Now she took a deep breath, girded her cynical loins, and turned slowly to look at herself in the full-length mirror hung on the back of her office door.

She closed her eyes. *Goodbye, romantic fool.* Then she took a deep breath and opened them.

Molly felt her attempt at cynicism dissolve with all the resistance of instant coffee granules meeting hot water. In fact everything dissolved: the clutter around her, the files that needed to be dealt with, the colorful sounds of the East Village awaking outside her open transom window, something called out harshly in Polish or Ukrainian, the sound of a delivery truck stopped nearby, a horn honking.

Molly stared at herself in the mirror. She had fully expected to see her romantic *fantasy* debunked. It would just be her, too tall, too skinny, redheaded and pale-faced Molly Michaels, in a fancy dress. Not changed by it. Certainly not *completed* by it.

Instead, a princess looked solemnly back at her. Her red hair, pulled out of its very professional upsweep by the entrapment inside the dress and the brief fray with the pearl, was stirred up, hissing with static, fiery and free. Her pale skin looked not washed out as she had thought it would against the sea of white but flawless, like porcelain. And her eyes shimmered green as Irish fields in springtime.

The cut of the dress had seemed virginal before she put it on. Now she could see the neckline was sinful and the rich fabric was designed to cling to every curve, making her look sensuous, red-hot and somehow *ready.*

"This is not the lesson I was hoping for," she told herself, the stern tone doing nothing to help her drag her eyes away from the vision in the mirror. She ordered herself to take off the dress, in that same easily ignored stern tone. Instead, she did an experimental pose, and then another.

"I would have made a beautiful bride!" she cried mournfully.

Annoyed with herself, and with her weakness—eager to get away from all the feelings of loss for dreams not fulfilled that this dress was stirring up in her—she reached back to undo the fastener that held the zipper shut. It was stuck fast.

And much as she did not like what she had just discovered about herself—romantic notions apparently hopelessly engrained in her character—she could not bring herself to damage the dress in order to get it off.

Molly tried to pull it over her head without the benefit of the zipper, but it was too tight to slip off and when she lowered it again, all she had accomplished was her hair caught hard in the seed pearls that encrusted the neckline of the dress again.

It was as if the dress—and her romantic notions—were letting her know their hold on her was not going to be so easily dismissed!

Her phone rang; the two distinct beeps of Vivian Saint Pierre, known to one and all as Miss Viv, beloved founder of Second Chances. Miss Viv and Molly were always the first two into the office in the morning.

Instead of answering the phone, Molly headed out of her own office and down the hall to her boss's office to be rescued.

From myself, she acknowledged wryly.

Miss Viv would look at this latest predicament Molly had gotten herself into, know instantly *why* Molly had been compelled to put on the dress and then as she was undoing the zip she would say something wise and comforting about Molly's shattered romantic hopes.

Miss Viv had never liked Chuck Howard, Molly's fiancé. When Molly had arrived at work that day six months ago with her ring finger empty, Miss Viv had nodded approvingly and said, "You're well rid of that ne'er-do-well."

And that was even before Molly had admitted that her bank account was as empty as her ring finger!

That was exactly the kind of pragmatic attention Molly needed when a dress like this one was trying to undo all the lessons she was determined to take from her broken engagement!

With any luck, by the end of the day her getting stuck in the dress would be nothing more than an office joke.

Determined to carry off the lighthearted laugh at herself, she burst through the door of Miss

Viv's office after a single knock, the wedding march humming across her lips.

But a look at Miss Viv, sitting behind her desk, stopped Molly in her tracks. The hum died mid-note. Miss Viv did not look entertained by the theatrical entrance. She looked horrified.

And when her gaze slid away from where Molly stood in the doorway to where a chair was nearly hidden behind the open door, Molly's breath caught and she slowly turned her head.

Despite the earliness of the hour, Miss Viv was not alone!

A man sat in the chair behind the door, the only available space for visitors in Miss Viv's hopelessly disorganized office.

No, not just a man. The kind of man that every woman dreamed of walking down the aisle toward.

The man sitting in Miss Viv's office was not just handsome, he was breathtaking. In a glance, Molly saw neat hair as rich as dark chocolate, firm lips, a strong chin with the faintest hint of a cleft, a nose saved from perfection—but made unreasonably more attractive—by the slight crook of an old break and a thin scar running across the bridge of it.

The aura of confidence, of *success,* was underscored by how exquisitely he was dressed. He was in a suit of coal-gray, obviously custom tailored. He had on an ivory shirt, a silk tie also in shades of gray. The ensemble would have been totally conservative had it not been for how it all matched the gray shades of his eyes. The cut of the clothes emphasized rather than hid the pure power of his build.

The power was underscored in the lines of his face.

And especially in the light in his eyes. The surprise that widened them did not cover the fact he radiated a kind of self-certainty, a cool confidence, that despite the veneer of civilization he wore so well, reminded Molly of a gunslinger.

In fact, that was the color of those eyes, *exactly,* gunmetal-gray, something in them watchful, *waiting.* She shivered with awareness. Despite the custom suit, the Berluti shoes, the Rolex that glinted at his wrist, he was the kind of man who sat with his back to the wall, always facing the door.

The man radiated power and the set of his shoulders telegraphed the fact that, unlike Chuck, this man was pure strength. The word *excuse* would not appear in his vocabulary.

No, Molly could tell by the fire in his eyes that if the ship was going down, or the building was on fire—if the town needed saving and he had just ridden in on his horse—he was the one you would follow, he was the one you would rely on to save you.

An aggravating conclusion since she was so newly committed to relying on herself, her career and her coworkers to save her from a disastrous life of unremitting loneliness. The little featherless budgie she had at home—the latest in a long list of loving strays that had populated her life—also helped.

The little *swish* of attraction she felt for the stranger made her current situation even more annoying. It didn't matter how much he looked like the perfect person to cast in the center of a romantic fantasy! She had given up on such twaddle! She was well on her way to becoming one of those women perfectly comfortable sitting at an outdoor café, alone, sipping a fine glass of wine and reading a book. Not even slipping a look at the male passers-by!

Of course, this handsome devil appearing without warning in her boss's office on a Monday morning was a test, just like the dress. It was a test of her commitment to the new and independent Molly Michaels, a test of her ability to separate her imaginings from reality.

Look at her deciding he was the one you would follow in a catastrophe when she knew absolutely nothing about him except that he had an exceedingly handsome face. Molly reminded herself, extra sternly, that all the catastrophes in her life had been of her own making. Besides, with the kind of image he portrayed—all easy self-assurance and leashed sexuality—probably more than one woman had built fantasies of hope and forever around him. He was of an age where if he wanted to be taken he would be. And if his ring finger—and the expression on his face as he looked at the dress—was any indication, he was not!

"Sorry," Molly said to Miss Viv, "I thought you were alone." She gave a quick, curt nod of acknowledgment to the stranger, making sure to strip any remaining *hopeless dreamer* from herself before she met his eyes.

"But, Molly, when I rang your office, I wanted you to come, and you must have wanted something?" Miss Viv asked her before she made her escape.

Usually imaginative, Molly drew a blank for explaining away her attire and she could think of not a single reason to be here except the truth.

"The zip is stuck, but I can manage. Really. Excuse me." She was trying to slide back out the door when his eyes narrowed on her.

"Is your hair caught in the dress?"

His voice was at least as sensual as the silk where the dress caressed her naked skin.

Molly could feel her cheeks turning a shade of red that was probably going to put her hair to shame.

"A little," she said proudly. "It's nothing.

Excuse me." She tried to lift her chin, to prove how *nothing* it was, but her hair was caught hard enough that she could not, and she also could not prevent a little wince of pain as the movement caused the stuck hair to yank at her tender scalp.

"That looks painful," he said quietly, getting to his feet with that casual grace one associated with athletes, the kind of ease of movement that disguised how swift they really were. But he was swift, because he was standing in front of her before she could gather her wits and make good her escape.

The smart thing to do would be to step back as he took that final step toward her. But she was astounded to find herself rooted to the spot, paralyzed, helpless to move away from him.

The world went very still. It seemed as if all the busy activity on the street outside ceased, the noises faded, the background and Miss Viv melted into a fuzzy kaleidoscope as the stranger leaned in close to her.

With the ease born of supreme confidence in himself—as if he performed this kind of rescue on a daily basis—he lifted the pressure of the dress up off her shoulder with one hand, and with the other, he carefully unwound her hair from the pearls they were caught in.

Given that outlaw remoteness in his eyes, he was unbelievably gentle, his fingers unhurried in her hair.

Molly's awareness of him was nothing less than shocking, his nearness tingling along her skin, his touch melting parts of her that she had hoped were turned to ice permanently.

The moment took way too long. And not nearly long enough. His concentration was complete, the intensity of his steely-gray gaze as he dealt with her tangled hair, his unsettling nearness, the graze of his fingers along her neck, stealing her breath.

At least Molly didn't feel as if she was breathing, but then she realized she must, indeed, be pulling air in and out, because she could smell him.

His scent was wonderful, bitingly masculine, good aftershave, expensive soap, freshly pressed linen.

Molly gazed helplessly into his face, unwill-
ingly marveling at the chiseled perfection of his
features, the intrigue of the faint crook in his
nose, the white line of that scar, the brilliance
of his eyes. He, however, was pure focus, as if
the only task that mattered to him was freeing
her hair from the remaining pearl that held it
captive.

Apparently he was not marveling at the circumstances that had brought his hands to her
hair and the soft place on her neck just below
her ear, apparently he was not swamped by
their scents mingling nor was he fighting a
deep awareness that a move of a mere half inch
would bring them together, full frontal contact,
the swell of her breast pressing into the hard
line of his chest...

The dress, suddenly freed, fell back onto her
shoulder. He actually smiled then, the faintest
quirk of a gorgeous mouth, and she felt herself
floundering in the depths of stormy sea eyes, the
chill gray suddenly illuminated by the sun.

"Did you say the zipper was stuck as well?"
he asked.

Oh, God. Had she said that? She could not prolong this encounter! It was much more of a test of the new confidently-sitting-at-the-café-alone her than she was ready for!

But mutely, caught in a spell, she turned her back to him and stood stock-still, waiting. She shivered at the thought of a wedding night, what this moment meant, and at the same time that unwanted thought seeped warmly into her brain, he touched her.

She felt the slight brush of his hand, again, on delicate skin, this time at the back of her neck. Her senses were so intensely engaged that she heard the faint pop of the hook parting from the eye. She registered the feel of his hand, felt astounded by the hard, unyielding texture of his skin.

He looked like he was pure business, a banker maybe, a wealthy benefactor, but there was nothing soft about his hand that suggested a life behind a desk, his tools a phone and a computer. For some reason it occurred to her that hands like that belonged to people who handled ropes…range riders, mountain climbers.

Pirates. Ah, yes, pirates with all that mysterious charm.

He dispensed with the hook at the top of the zipper in a split second, a man who had dispensed with such delicate items many times? And then he paused, apparently realizing the height of the zipper would make it nearly impossible for her to manage the rest by herself—she hoped he would not consider how much determination it had taken her to get it up in the first place—and then slid the zipper down a sensuous inch or two.

With that same altered sense of alertness Molly could feel cool air on that small area of her newly exposed naked back, and then, though she did not glance back, she could feel heat. His gaze? Her own jumbled thoughts?

Molly fought the chicken in her that just wanted to bolt out the open door. Instead, she turned and faced him.

"There you go," he said mildly, rocking back on his heels. The heat must have come from her own badly rattled thoughts, because his eyes were cool, something veiled in their intriguing silver depths.

"Thank you," she said, struggling to keep her voice deliberately controlled to match the look in his eyes. "I'm sorry to interrupt."

"No, no, Molly," Miss Viv said, and it was a mark of the intensity of her encounter with him that Molly was actually jarred by the fact Miss Viv was still in the room. "I called your office to invite you to meet Mr. Whitford. I'm going on an unscheduled holiday, and Mr. Whitford is taking the helm."

Molly felt the shock of Miss Viv's announcement ripple down a spine that had already been thoroughly shocked this morning. But even as she dealt with the shock, part of her mused with annoying dreaminess, *helm. Pirate. I knew it.*

"Houston Whitford, Molly Michaels," Miss Viv said. The introduction seemed ridiculously formal considering the rather astounding sense of intimacy Molly had just felt under his touch.

Still, now she felt duty-bound to extend her hand, and be touched again, even as she was digesting the fact *he* was in charge. How could that be? Molly was always in charge when Miss Viv was away!

And Miss Viv was going on a holiday, but hadn't told anyone? Second Chances was a family and far better than Molly's family of origin at providing a place that was safe, and supportive, and rarely unpredictable.

"There are going to be a few changes," Miss Viv said, cheerfully, as if Molly's nice safe world was in no way being threatened. "And no one is more qualified to make them than Mr. Whitford. I expect Second Chances is going to blossom, absolutely go to the next level, under his leadership. I'm thrilled to pass the reins to him."

But Molly felt the threat of her whole world shifting. Miss Viv was stepping down? The feeling only intensified when Houston Whitford's hand—warm, strong, cool—touched her skin again. His hand enveloped her hand and despite the pure professionalism of his shake, the hardness of his grip told her something, as did the glittering silver light in his eyes.

He was not the usual kind of person who worked an ill-paying job at a charity. His suit said something his hands did not: that he was used to a world of higher finances, higher-power, higher-tech.

The only thing that was higher at Second Chances was the satisfaction, the feeling of changing the world for the better.

The cost of his suit probably added up to their operating budget for a month! He didn't fit the cozy, casual and rather shabby atmosphere of the Second Chances office at all.

She felt the unmistakable tingle of pure danger all along her spine. There was something about Houston Whitford that was not adding up. Change followed a man like that as surely as pounding rain followed the thunderstorm.

Molly, her father had said, on the eve of leaving their family home forever, *there is going to be a change.*

And she had been allergic to that very thing ever since! She wanted her world to be safe and unchanging and that view had intensified after she had flirted with a major life change in the form of Chuck. Since then Second Chances had become more her safe haven than ever.

"What kind of changes?" she asked Miss Viv now, failing to keep a certain trepidation from entering her voice.

"Mr. Whitford will be happy to brief you, um, after you've changed into something more appropriate," Miss Viv said, and then glanced at her watch. "Oh, my! I do have a plane to catch. I'm going to a spa in Arizona, my dear."

"You're going to a spa in Arizona, and you didn't tell anyone?" It seemed unimaginable. That kind of vacation usually should have entailed at least a swimsuit shopping excursion together!

"The opportunity came up rather suddenly," Miss Viv said, unapologetically thrilled. "A bolt from the blue, an unexpected gift from an old friend."

Molly tried to feel delighted for her. No one deserved a wonderful surprise more than her boss.

"For how long?" she asked.

But the shameful truth was Molly did not feel

delighted at her boss's good fortune. *Sudden change*. Molly hated that kind more than the regular variety.

"Two weeks," Miss Viv said with a sigh of anticipated delight.

Two weeks? Molly wanted to shout. *That was ridiculous. People went to spas for a few hours, maybe a few days, never two weeks!*

"But when you come back, everything will be back to normal?" Molly pressed.

Miss Viv laughed. "Oh, sweetie," she said. "What is normal? A setting on a clothes dryer as far as I'm concerned."

Molly stared at her boss. What was normal? Not something to be joked about! It was what Molly had never had. She'd never had a normal family. Her engagement had certainly not been normal. It felt as if she had spent a good deal of her life searching for it, and coming up short. Even her pets were never normal.

Molly's life had been populated with the needy kind of animal that no one else wanted. A dog with three legs, a cat with no meow. Her current resident was a bald budgie, his scrawny body devoid of feathers.

"I've been thinking of retiring," Miss Viv shocked Molly further by saying. "So, who knows? After the two weeks is up, we'll just play it by ear."

Molly wanted to protest that she didn't like playing it by ear. She liked plans and schedules, calendars that were marked for months in advance.

If Miss Viv retired, would Houston Whitford be in charge forever?

She could not think of a way of asking that did not show her dread at the prospect!

Besides, there is no *forever,* Molly reminded herself. That was precisely why she had put on this dress. To debunk *forever* myths.

She particularly did not want to entertain *that* word anywhere near the vicinity of him, a man whose faintest touch could make a woman's vows of self-reliance disintegrate like foundations crumbling at the first tremor of the coming quake.

CHAPTER TWO

THE bride flounced out of the room, and unbidden, words crowded into Houston's brain.

And then they lived happily ever after.

He scoffed at himself, and the words. Yes, it was true that a dress like that, filled out by a girl like Molly Michaels, represented a fairy tale.

But the fact she was stuck in it, the zipper stubborn, her hair wound painfully around the pearls, represented more the reality: relationships of the romantic variety were sticky, complicated, *entrapping.*

Besides, a man didn't come from the place Houston Whitford had come from and believe in fairy tales. He believed in his own strength, his own ability to survive. He saw the cynicism with which he had regarded that dress as a *gift.*

In fact, the unexpected appearance of one of the Second Chances employees in full wedding regalia only confirmed what several weeks of research had already told him.

Second Chances reminded Houston, painfully, of an old-style family operated bookstore. Everyone was drawn to the warmth of it, it was always crowded and full of laughter and discussion, but when it came time to actually buy a book it could not compete with the online giants, streamlined, efficient, economical. Just how Houston liked his businesses, running like well-oiled machines. No brides, no ancient, adorable little old ladies at the helm.

He fought an urge to press the scar over the old break on the bridge of his nose. It ached unbearably lately. Had it ached ever since, in a rare moment of weakness, he had agreed to help out here? This wasn't his kind of job. He dealt in reality, in cold, hard fact. Where did a poorly run charity, with brides in the hallways and octogenarians behind the desks, fit into his world?

"And that was our Molly," Miss Viv said brightly. "Isn't she lovely?"

"Lovely," Houston managed. He recalled part two of his mission here.

Miss Viv had confessed to him she was thinking of retiring. She loved Molly and considered her her natural successor. But she was a little worried. She wanted his opinion on whether Molly was too soft-hearted for the job.

"Is she getting ready for her wedding?" On the basis of their very brief encounter, Molly Michaels seemed the kind of woman that a man who was not cynical and jaded like him—a man who believed in fairy tales, love ever after, family—would snatch up.

He didn't even like the direction of those thoughts. The wedding dress should only be viewed in the context of the job he had to do here. What was Miss Michaels doing getting ready for her wedding at work? How did that reflect on a future for her in management?

The job he hadn't wanted was getting less attractive by the second. A demand of complete professionalism was high on his list of fixes for the ailing companies he put back on the track to success.

"She's not getting ready for her wedding," Miss Viv said with a sympathetic sigh. "The exact opposite, I'm afraid. Her engagement broke off before they even set a date. A blessing, though the poor child did not see it that way at the time. She's not been herself since it happened."

At this point, with anyone else, he would make it clear, right now, he didn't want to know a single thing about Molly Michaels's personal life. But this job was different than any he'd ever taken on before. And this was Miss Viv.

Everybody was a *poor child* to her. His need to analyze, to have answers to puzzles, surprised him by not filing this poor child information under strictly personal, none of his business, nothing to do with the job at hand. Instead, he allowed the question to form in his mind. *If a man believed in the fairy tale enough to ask someone like Molly Michaels to be his wife, why would he then be fool enough to let her get away?*

Because the truth was *lovely* was an unfortunate understatement, and would have been even before he had made the mistake of making the bridal vision somehow *real* by touching the heated silk of Molly's skin, the coiled copper of her hair.

Molly's eyes, the set of her sensuous mouth and the corkscrewing hair, not to mention the curves of a slender figure, had not really said *lovely* to him. Despite the fairy tale of the dress the word that had come to mind first was *sexy*.

Was that what had made him get up from his chair? Not really to rescue her from her obvious discomfort, but to see what was true about her? Sexy? Or innocent?

He was no Boy Scout, after all, not given to good deeds, which was another reason he should not be here at Second Chances.

Still, was his need to know that about Molly Michaels personal or professional? He had a feeling at Second Chances those lines had always been allowed to blur. *Note to self,* he thought wryly, *no more rescuing of damsels in distress.*

Though, really that was why he was here,

even if Miss Viv was obviously way too old to qualify as a damsel.

Houston Whitford was CEO of Precision Solutions, a company that specialized in rescuing ailing businesses, generally large corporations, from the brink of disaster. His position used all of his strengths, amongst which he counted a formidable ability to not be swayed be emotion.

He was driven, ambitious and on occasion, unapologetically ruthless, and he could see that was a terrible fit with Second Chances. He didn't really even *like* charities, cynically feeling that for one person to receive the charity of another was usually as humiliating for the person in need as it was satisfying for the one who could give.

But the woman who sat in front of him was a reminder that no man had himself alone to thank for his circumstances.

Houston Whitford was here, at Second Chances, because he owed a debt.

And he was here for the same reason he suspected most men blamed when they found themselves in untenable situations.

His mother, Beebee, had suggested he help out. So, it had already been personal, some line blurred, even before the bride had showed up.

Beebee was Houston's foster mother, but it was a distinction he rarely made. She had been there when his real mother—as always—had not. Beebee had been the first person he had ever felt genuinely cared about him and what happened to him. He owed his life as it was to her *charity,* and he knew it.

Miss Viv was Beebee's oldest friend, part of that remarkable group of women who had circled around a tough boy from a terrible neighborhood and seen something in him—*believed in something in him*—that no one had ever seen or believed in before.

You didn't say *sorry, too busy* in the face of that kind of a debt.

It had started a month ago, when he'd hosted a surprise birthday celebration for Beebee. The catered high tea had been held at his newly acquired "Gold Coast" condominium with its coveted Fifth Avenue address, facing Central Park.

Beebee and "the girls" had been all sparkle then, oohing over the white-gloved doorman, the luxury of the lobby, the elevators, the hallways. Inside the sleek interior of his eleven-million-dollar apartment, no detail had gone unremarked, from tiger wood hardwood to walnut moldings to the spectacular views.

But as the party had progressed, Miss Viv had brought up Second Chances, the charity she headed, and that all "the girls" supported. She confessed it was having troubles, financial and otherwise, that baffled her.

"Oh, Houston will help, won't you, dear?" his foster mom had said.

And all eyes had been on him, and in a blink he wasn't a successful entrepreneur who had proven himself over and over again, but that young ruffian, *poor child*, rescued from mean streets and a meaner life, desperately trying to live up to their expectation that he was really a good person under that tough exterior.

But after that initial weakness that had made

him say yes, he'd laid down the law. If they wanted his help, they would have to accept the fact he was doing it his way: no interfering from them, no bringing him home-baked good-ies to try to sway him into keeping things the very same way that had gotten the charity into trouble in the first place and *especially* no ref-erences to his past.

Of course, they hadn't understood that.

"But why ever not? We're all so proud of you, Houston!"

But Beebee and her friends weren't just proud of him because of who he was now. No, they were the ones who held in their memories that measuring stick of who he had once been…a troubled fourteen-year-old kid from the tene-ments of Clinton, a neighborhood that had once been called Hell's Kitchen.

They saw it as something to be admired that he had overcome his circumstances—his father being sent to prison, his mother abandoning him—but he just saw it as something left behind him.

Beebee and Miss Viv dispensed charity as

easily as they breathed, but as well-meaning as they were, they had no idea how shaming that part of his life, when he had been so needy and so vulnerable, was to him. He did not excuse himself because he had only been fourteen.

He still felt, sometimes, that he was their *poor child,* an object of pity that they had rescued and nursed back to wellness like a near-drowned kitten.

Was he insecure about his past? No, he didn't think so. But it was over and it was done. He'd always had an ability to place his life in neat compartments; his need for order did not allow for overlapping.

But suddenly, he thought of that letter that had arrived at his home last week, a cheap envelope and a prison postmark lying on a solid mahogany desk surely a sign that a man could not always keep his worlds from overlapping.

Houston had told no one about the arrival of that letter, not even the only other person who knew his complete history, Beebee.

Was that part of why he was sending her away with Miss Viv? Not just because he knew they could probably not resist sharing the titillating details of his past with anyone who would listen, including all the employees here at Second Chances, but because he didn't want to talk to Beebee about that letter? The thought of that letter, plus being here at Second Chances, made him feel what Houston Whitford hated feeling the most: *vulnerable,* as if that most precious of commodities, *control,* was slipping away from him.

And there was something about this place— the nature of charity, Miss Viv and his history, Molly, sweetly sensual in virginal white—that made him feel, not as if his guard was being let down, but that his bastions were being stormed.

He was a proud man. That pride had carried him through times when all else had failed. He didn't want Miss Viv's personal information about him undermining his authority to rescue her charity, changing the way people he had to deal with looked at him.

And when people found out his story, it did change the way they looked at him.

He could tell, for instance, Molly Michaels would fall solidly in the soft-hearted category. She'd love an opportunity to treat him like a kitten who had nearly drowned! And he wasn't having it.

"Let's discuss Molly Michaels for a minute," he said carefully. "I'd like to have a little talk with her about—"

"Don't be hard on her!" Miss Viv cried. "Try not to judge Molly for the outfit. She was just being playful. It was actually good to see that side of her again," Miss Viv said.

Playful. He liked playful. In the bedroom. In the office? Not so much.

"Please don't hurt her feelings," Miss Viv warned him.

Hurt her feelings? What did feelings have to do with running an organization, with expecting the best from it, with demanding excellence?

He did give in to the little impulse, then, to press the ridge of the scar along his nose.

Miss Viv's voice lowered into her *juicy-secret* tone. "The broken engagement? She's had a heartbreak recently."

It confirmed his wisdom in sending Miss Viv away for the duration of the Second Chances business makeover. He didn't want to know this, *at all.* He pressed harder. The ache along the scar line did not diffuse.

"A cad, I'm afraid," Miss Viv said, missing his every signal that he did not want to be any part of the office stories, the gossip, the personalities.

Despite his desire to remove himself from it, Houston felt a sudden and completely unexpected pulsing of fury.

Not for the circumstances he found himself in, certainly not at Miss Viv, who could not help herself. No, Houston felt an undisciplined desire to hurt a man he did not know for breaking the heart of a woman he also did not know—save for the exquisite tenderness of her neck beneath his fingertips.

That flash of unreasonable fury, an undisciplined reaction, was gone nearly as soon as it happened, but it still served to remind him that things did not always stay in their neat compartments. He had not overcome what he had come from as completely as everyone believed.

He came from a world where violence was the default reaction.

Houston knew if he was to let down his guard, lose his legendary sense of control for a second—one second—he could become that man his father had been, his carefully constructed world blown apart by forces—fury, passion—that could rise up in a storm that he had no hope of taming.

It was the reason Houston did not even allow himself to contemplate his life in the context of fairy tales represented by a young woman in a bridal gown. There was no room for a compartment like that in the neat, tidy box that made up his life.

There was a large compartment for work, an almost equally large one for his one and only passion, the combat sport of boxing.

There were smaller compartments for his social obligations, for Beebee, for occasional and casual relationships with the rare member of the opposite sex who shared his aversion for commitment. There were some compartments that were nailed shut.

But now the past was not staying in the neat compartment system. The compartment that held Houston's father *and* his mother was being pried up, despite the nails trying to hold it firmly shut.

Houston's father had written his only son a letter that asked nothing and expected nothing. And yet at the same time Houston was bitterly aware that how he reacted to it would prove who he really was.

After nineteen years, his father was getting out of prison.

And it felt as if all those years of Houston outdistancing his past had been a total waste of energy. Because there it was, waiting for him, right around the next bend in time.

The scar across his nose flared with sudden pain, and Houston pressed a finger into the line of the old break, aware he was entering a danger zone that the mean streets of Clinton had nothing on.

* * *

"Have a seat," Houston invited Molly several hours later, after he had personally waved good-bye to Beebee and Miss Viv at the airport.

"Thank you." She took a seat, folded her hands primly in her lap and looked at him expectantly.

It was his second encounter with her, and he was determined it was going to go differently than the first. It was helpful that Miss Viv was not there smiling at him as if he was her favorite of all charity cases.

And it was helpful that Molly Michaels was all business now, no remnant of the blushing bride she had been anywhere in sight. No, she was dressed in a conservative slack suit, her amazing hair pinned sternly up on her head.

Still, it was way too easy to remember how it had felt underneath his hands. He was not going to allow himself to contemplate the fact that even after untangling her from that dress several hours ago he was no closer to knowing her truth: was she sexy? Or innocent?

Not thoughts that were strictly *professional*.

In fact, those were exactly the kind of thoughts that made a man crazy.

"I'm sorry about the dress. You must think I'm crazy."

Damn her for using that word!

The nails holding a compartment of Houston's past shut gave an outrageous squeak. Houston remembered the senior Whitford had been made *crazy* by a beautiful woman, Houston's mother.

Who hadn't she made crazy? Beautiful, but untouchable. Both of them had loved her desperately, a fact that had only seemed to amuse her, allowed her to toy with her power over them. The truth? Houston would have robbed a bank for her, too, if he'd thought it would allow him to finally win something from her.

The memory, unwanted, of his craving for something his mother had been unable to give made him feel annoyed with himself.

"Crazy?" he said. *You can't begin to know the meaning of the word.* "Let's settle for eccentric."

She blushed, and his reaction was undisciplined, *unprofessional,* a ridiculous desire, like a juvenile boy, to find out what made her blush and then to make it happen *often.*

"So, you've been here how long?" Houston asked, even though he knew, just to get himself solidly back on the professional track.

"As an employee for several years. But I actually started here as a volunteer during high school."

Again, unprofessional thoughts tickled at him: what had she been like during high school? The popular girl? The sweet geek? *Would she have liked him?*

Houston remembered an incident from his own high school years. She probably would not have liked him, *at all.* He shook off the memory like a pesky fly. High school? That was fifteen years ago! That was the problem with things coming out of their compartments. They could become unruly, pop up unannounced, uninvited, in moments when his concentration was challenged, when his attention drifted.

Which was rarely, thank God.

Since the memories had come, though, he

exercised cool discipline over them. He reminded himself that good things could come from bad. His mother's abandonment had ultimately opened the door to a different world for him; the high school "incident" had led to Beebee putting him in boxing classes "to channel his aggression."

Houston was more careful than most men with the word *love,* but he thought he could honestly say he loved the combat sport of boxing, the absolute physical challenge of it, from the grueling cardiovascular warm-up to punching the heavy bags and the speed bags, practicing the stances, the combinations, the jabs and the hooks. He occasionally sparred, but awareness of the unexpected power of fury prevented him from taking matches.

Now he wondered if a defect in character like fury could lie dormant, spring back to life when it was least expected.

No, he snapped at himself.

Yes, another voice answered when a piece of Molly's hair sprang free of the restraints she had pinned it down with, curled down the soft line of her temple.

She'd been engaged to a cad.

Tonight, he told himself sternly, he would punch straight left and right combinations into the heavy bag until his hands, despite punch mitts, ached from it. Until his whole body hurt and begged for release. For now he would focus, not on her hair or her past heartbreaks, but on the job he was here to do.

Houston realized Molly's expression had turned quizzical, wondered how much of the turmoil of that memory he had just had he had let slip over his usually well-schooled features.

Did she look faintly sympathetic? Had she seen something he didn't want her to see? Good grief, had Miss Viv managed to let something slip about him?

Whatever, he knew just how to get rid of that look on her face, the look of a woman who *lived* to make the world softer and better.

A cad could probably spot that gentle, compassion-filled face from a mile away! It would be good for her to toughen up.

"Let me be very blunt," he said, looking at the papers in front of him instead of her hair, the delicate creamy skin at her throat. "Second Chances is in a lot of trouble. I need to turn things around and I need to do it fast."

"Second Chances is in trouble?" Molly was genuinely astounded. "But how? The second-hand stores that provide the majority of our funding seem to do well."

"They do perform exceedingly well. The problem seems to be in an overextension of available funds. Your department?"

Here it was: could she make the kind of hard decisions that would be required of her if she took over the top spot in the newly revamped Second Chances?

The softness left her face, replaced with wariness. Better than softness in terms of her managerial abilities. If that was good, why did he feel so bad?

"You can't run an organization that brings in close to a million dollars a year like a mom and pop store. You can't give everyone who comes in here with their hand out and a hard luck story everything they ask for."

"I don't!" she said. "I'm very careful what I fund."

He saw her flinch from his bluntness, but at this crucial first stage there was no other way to prepare people for the changes that had to happen. Another little curl broke free of her attempt to tame her hair, and he watched it, sentenced himself to another fifteen minutes on the bag and forged on.

"Two thousand dollars to the Flatbush Boys Choir travel fund? There is no Flatbush Boys Choir."

"I know that now," she said, defensively. "I had just started here. Six of them came in. The most adorable little boys in matching sweaters. They even sang a song for me."

"Here's a check written annually to the Bristol Hall Ladies' Lunch Group. No paperwork. No report. Is there a Bristol Hall Ladies' Lunch Group? What do they do? When do they meet? Why do they get money for lunch?"

"That was grandfathered in from before I started. Miss Viv looks after it."

"So, you're project manager, except when Miss Viv takes over?"

"She is the boss," Molly said uneasily, her defensive tone a little more strident.

"Ah." He studied her for a moment, then said softly, "Look, I'm not questioning your competence."

She looked disbelieving. Understandably.

"It's just that some belt-tightening is going to have to happen. What I need from you as I do research, review files and talk to people is for you to go over your programming in detail. I need exact breakdowns on how you choose programs. I need to review your budgets, I need to analyze your monitoring systems."

She looked like she had been hit by a tank. Now would be the wrong time to remember the sweet softness of her skin under his fingertips, how damned protective he had felt when he heard about the *cad*. Now he was the cad!

"How soon can you have that to me?" he pressed.

"A week?"

A chief executive officer needed to work faster, make decisions more quickly. "You have until tomorrow morning."

She glared at him. That was good. Much easier to defend against than sweet, shocked vulnerability. The angry spark in her eyes could almost make him forget her hair, that tender place at her nape. Almost.

He plunged forward, eager to get the barriers—compromised by hands in hair—back up where they belonged. Eager to find out what he needed to know about her—professionally—so he could make a recommendation when the job here was done and move on.

"I've been sorting through paperwork for a number of weeks," he told her. "I have to tell you, after a brief look, it's quite evident to me that you're going to have to ax some of your projects. Sooner rather than later. I've short-listed a few that are on the block."

"Ax projects?" she said with disbelief. "Some of *my* projects are on the block?"

He nodded. He felt not the least like a knight

riding in to rescue the business in distress. Or the damsel. He was causing distress, in fact. The feeling of being the cad intensified even though he knew in the long run this would pay off for Second Chances, guarantee their good health and success in the coming years and possibly decades if this was done right, if they had the right leader to move ahead with.

"Which ones?" She went so pale a faint dusting of freckles appeared over the bridge of her nose.

He was annoyed that his feeling of being the cad only deepened, and that she was acting as if he had asked her to choose one of her children to float down the river in a basket. He was aware of feeling the faintest twinge of a foreign emotion, which after a second or two he identified, with further annoyance, as guilt.

Houston Whitford did not feel guilty about doing his job! Satisfied, driven, take charge, in control. Of course, generally, it would be fairly safe to say he didn't *feel,* period.

He used a reasonable tone of voice, designed to convince either her or himself that of course he was not a cad! "We have to make some practical decisions for the future of this organization."

She looked unconvinced about his cad status, and the careful use of the *we* did not even begin to make her think they were a team.

She looked mutinous, then stunned, then mutinous again. Her face was an open book of emotion.

"Is it that bad?" she finally sputtered. "How can it be? Miss Viv never said a word. She didn't even seem worried when she left!"

He had actually sheltered Miss Viv from how bad things were as he had begun to slug his way through the old gal's abysmal record and bookkeeping systems. Miss Viv—and his mother, Second Chances's largest patron—trusted him to fix this. He would. Neither of them needed to know the extent he had to go to. But Molly Michaels did, since the mantle of it all could quite possibly fall on her slender shoulders.

"Yes, it's bad." He closed the fuchsia cover on one of the project reports, the mauve one on another and put those files on the desk between them. "The Easter Egg hunt is gone. The poetry competition is out. And I'm looking at the prom dress thing, and—"

"Prom Dreams?" she gasped. "You can't! You don't know what it means to those girls."

"Have you ever known real hardship?" he asked her, his voice deliberately cold. This job was not going to be easy no matter how he did it. Hard choices had to be made. And he had to see if she was willing to make them. There was no way she was going to be suited to taking over the top job at Second Chances if she was always going to be blinded by the stars in her eyes.

But cad that he was, his gaze went to the lip that she was nibbling with distraction. He was shocked that out of the blue he wondered if one of his hard choices was not going to be whether or not to taste those luscious lips before he made his escape!

She met his eyes. Stopped nibbling. Things that should be simple, cut-and-dried, suddenly seemed complicated. He wished she wasn't looking at him as if she was remembering, too, that unguarded moment when two strangers had touched and the potential for something wild and unpredictable had arced in the air between them.

"My parents divorced when I was young," she offered, softly. "I considered that a terrible hardship. The only one I've known, but life altering."

Thank God she didn't mention the cad! He could see the pain in her eyes. Houston reminded himself, sternly, that he likely had a genetic predisposition toward allowing women to make him crazy. Because he had no business thinking of trying to change the light in her eyes. But he was thinking of it, of how soft her lips would be beneath his own.

Why would that genetic predisposition toward *crazy* be surfacing now, for God's sake? He'd been around many, many beautiful women. He'd always taken his ability to keep his emotional distance for granted, one of the few gifts from his chaotic childhood.

Don't form attachments. Don't care too deeply.

Except for his business and boxing. Both

had rigid guidelines and rules that if followed, produced a predictable result. That made them safe things to care about. An occasional bruised knuckle or fat lip, a skirmish in the business world, those hazards were nothing compared to the minefields of becoming attached to people, where the results were rarely predictable.

No, he knew exactly where he was going to channel his substantial passion and energy.

He was being drawn backward, feeling shadows from his past falling over him, entirely against his will. He blamed the letter from his father and the unfortunate fact it coincided with the past weeks of going over files of people who were as desperate and as needy as his family had once been.

It was his annoyance at himself for allowing those thoughts into his business world that made his tone even sharper than it had to be, even if he was testing her ability to run a million dollar corporation.

"Have you ever been hungry?" But even as he asked it, he knew that question, too, stemmed not so much from professional interest as from a dark past he thought he had left behind.

"No," she said, "but I think I can imagine the desperation of it."

"Can you?" he said cynically.

Without warning a memory popped over the barrier of the thick, high wall he had constructed around the compartment of his childhood.

So hungry. Not a crumb of food in the house. Going into Sam's, the bakery at the corner of his street, Houston's heart beating a horrible tattoo in his chest, his mouth watering from the smells and the sights of the freshly baked bread. Looking around, it was crowded, no one paying any attention to him. Sam's back turned. Houston's hands closing around one of the still-warm loafs in a basket outside the counter, stuffing it under his thin jacket. Lifting his eyes to see Sam looking straight at him. And then Sam turning away, saying nothing, and Houston feeling the shame of the baker's pity so strongly he could not eat the bread. He brought it home to his mother, who had been indifferent to the offering, uncaring of what it had cost him.

Molly was looking at him, understandably perplexed by the question.

Stop it, he ordered himself. But another question came out anyway, clipped with unexpected anger. "Out of work?"

"I don't suppose the summer I chose to volunteer here instead of taking a paying job counts, does it?"

"The fact you could make a choice to volunteer instead of work indicates to me you have probably not known real hardship."

"That doesn't make me a bad person!" she said sharply. "Or unqualified for my job!"

"No," he said, taking a deep breath, telling himself to smarten up. "Of course it doesn't. I'm just saying your frame of reference when choosing projects may not take into account the harsh realities the people you are helping live with."

Another memory popped over that wall. His father drunk, belligerent, out of work again. Not his fault. Never his fault. His mother scream-

ing at his father. You loser. The look on his father's face. Rage. The flying fists, the breaking glass.

Houston could feel his heart beating as rapidly as though it had just happened. Molly was watching him, silently, the dismay and anger that had been in her face fading, becoming more thoughtful.

He ordered himself, again, to stop this. It was way too personal. But, master of control that he was, he did not stop.

"Have you ever had no place to live?"

"Of course not!"

Homelessness was so far from her reality that she could not even fathom it happening to her. Not that he had any right to treat that as a character defect, just because it had once been part of his childhood reality.

The eviction notice pounded onto the door. The hopeless feeling of nowhere to go and no place to feel safe. That sense that even that place he had called home was only an illusion. A sense that would be confirmed as the lives of the Whitfords spiraled steadily downward toward disaster.

Again Molly was silent, but her eyes were huge and had darkened to a shade of green that reminded him of a cool pond on a hot day, a place that promised refuge and rest, escape from a sizzling hot pressure-cooker of a world.

Her expression went from defensive to quiet. She studied his face, her own distress gone, as if she saw something in him, focused on something in him. He didn't want her to see his secrets, and yet something in her steady gaze made him feel seen, vulnerable.

"You're dealing with desperation, and you're doling out prom dresses? Are you kidding me?"

Houston was being way too harsh. He drew a deep breath, ordered himself to apologize, to back track, but suddenly the look on her face transformed. Her expression went from that quiet thoughtfulness to something much worse. *Knowing.*

He felt as transparent as a sheet of glass.

"You've known those things, haven't you?" she guessed softly.

The truth was he would rather run through Central Park in the buff than reveal himself emotionally.

He was stunned that she had seen right through his exquisite suit, all the trappings of wealth and success, seen right through the harshness of his delivery to what lay beneath.

He was astounded that a part of him—a weak part—*wanted* to be seen. Completely.

He didn't answer her immediately. The part of him that felt as if it was clamoring to be acknowledged quieted, and he came back to his senses.

He had to apply his own rules right now, to set an example for her. Don't form attachments. Don't care too deeply. Not about people. Not about programs.

And he needed to take away that feeling he'd been *seen*. Being despised for his severity felt a whole lot safer than that look she'd just given him.

He was laying down the law. If she didn't like

it, too bad. It was his job to see if she was capable of doing what needed to be done. Miss Viv wanted to hand this place over to her. There was absolutely no point doing any of this if six months later soft hearts had just run it back into the ground.

"Prom Dreams is gone," he said coolly. "It's up to you to get rid of it."

She bit her lip. She looked at her shoes. She glanced back at him, and tears were stinging her eyes.

There was no room for crying at work!

And absolutely no room for the way it made him feel: as if he wanted to fix it. For Pete's sake, he was the one who'd created it!

"I can see we are going to have a problem," he said. "You are a romantic. And I am a realist."

For a moment she studied him. For a moment he thought she would not be deflected by Prom Dreams, by his harshness, that despite it she would pursue what he had accidentally shown her.

But she didn't.

"I am not a romantic!" she protested.

"Anyone who shows up for work in a wedding gown is a romantic," he said, pleased with how well his deflection had worked. It was about her now, not about him, not about what experiences he did or didn't know.

"I didn't arrive in it," she said, embarrassed and faintly defensive, again. "It was a donation. It had been put on my desk."

"So naturally you had no alternative but to try it on."

"Exactly. I was just checking it for damage."

"Uh-huh," he said, not even trying to hide his skepticism. "Anyone who wants to buy dresses instead of feeding people is a romantic."

"It's not that black and white!"

"Everything is black and white to a realist. Rose-colored to a romantic."

"I might have been a romantic once," she said, her chin tilted proudly, "but I'm not anymore."

Ah, the cad. He shoved his hands under his desk when they insisted on forming fists.

"Good," he said, as if he were the most reasonable of men. "Then you should have no problem getting on board for the kind of pragmatic changes that need to be made around here."

He knew she was kidding herself about not being a romantic. Despite the recent heartbreak Miss Viv had told him about, it seemed that Molly had hopes and dreams written all over her. Could she tame that enough to do the job Second Chances needed her to do?

"Couldn't we look at ways to increase funding, rather than cutting programs?"

Ah, that's what he wanted to hear. Realistic ideas for dealing with problems, creative approaches to solutions, coming at challenges from different directions, experimenting with angles.

For the first time, he thought *maybe*. Maybe Molly Michaels had the potential to run the show. But he let nothing of that optimism into his voice. It was just too early to tell. Because it couldn't work if she was so attached to things that she could not let go of the ones that were dragging the organization down.

"Believe me, I'm looking at everything. That's my job. But I still want every single thing Second

Chances funds to have merit, to be able to undergo the scrutiny of the people I will be approaching for funding, and to pass with flying colors."

"I think," she said, slowly, "our different styles might work together, not against each other, if we gave them a chance."

He frowned at that. He wasn't looking for a partnership. He wasn't looking to see if they could work together. He wanted to evaluate whether she could work alone. He wasn't looking for anything to complicate what needed to be done here. It already was way too complicated.

Memories. Unexpected emotion.

Annoyed with himself, he put Houston Whitford, CEO of Precision Solutions, solidly back in the driver's seat.

"What needs to be done is pretty cut-and-dried," Houston said. "I've figured it out on paper, run numbers, done my homework. A team of experts is coming in here tomorrow to implement changes. Second Chances needs computer experts, business analysts, accounting wizards. It needs an image face-lift. It needs to be run like a corporation, stream-lined, professional."

"A corporation?" she said, horrified. "This is a family!"

"And like most families, it's dysfunctional." *That* was the Houston Whitford he knew and loved.

"What a terribly cynical thing to say!"

Precisely. And every bit of that cynicism had been earned in the school of hard knocks. "If you want Walt Disney, you go to the theater or rent *Old Yeller* from the video store. I deal in reality."

"You don't think the love and support of a family is possible in the business environment?"

The brief hope he'd felt about Molly's suitability to have Miss Viv turn over the reins to her was waning.

"That would assume that the love and support of family is a reality, not a myth. Miss Michaels, there is no place for sentiment in the corporate world."

"You're missing all that is important about Second Chances!"

"Maybe, for the first time, someone is seeing exactly what *is* important about Second Chances. Survival. That would speak to the bottom line. Which at the moment is a most unbecoming shade of red."

She eyed him, and for a moment anger and that other thing—that soft *knowing*—warred in her beautiful face. He pleaded with the anger to win. Naturally, the way his day was going, it didn't.

"Let me show you *my* Second Chances before you make any decisions about the programs," she implored. "You've seen them in black and white, on paper, but there's more to it than that. I want to show you the soul of this organiza-tion."

He sighed. "The soul of it? And you're not romantic? Organizations don't have souls."

"The best ones do. Second Chances does," she said with determination. "And you need to see that."

Don't do it, he ordered himself.

But suddenly it seemed like a life where a man was offered a glimpse at soul and refused it was a bereft place, indeed. Not that he was convinced she could produce such a glimpse. Romantics had a tendency to see things that weren't there. But realists didn't. Why not give her a chance to defend her vision? Really, could there be a better way to see if she had what it took to run Second Chances?

Still, he would have to spend time with her. More time than he had expected. And he didn't want to. And yet he did.

But if he did go along with her, once he had seen she was wrong, he could move forward, guilt-free. Make his recommendations about her future leadership, begin the job of cutting what needed to be cut. Possibly he wouldn't even feel like a cad when he axed Prom Dreams.

Besides, if there was one lesson he had carried forward when he'd left his old life behind him, it was to never show fear. Or uncertainty. The mean streets fed on fear.

No, you set your shoulders and walked straight

toward what you feared, unflinching, ready to battle it.

He feared the *knowing* that had flashed in her eyes, the place that had called to him like a cool, green pond to a man who had unknowingly been living on the searing hot sands of the desert. If he went there could he ever go back to where—to what—he had been before?

That was his fear and he walked toward it.

He shrugged, not an ounce of his struggle in his controlled voice. He said, "Okay. I'll give you a day to convince me."

"Two."

He leaned back in his chair, studied her, thought it was probably very unwise to push this thing by spending two days in close proximity to her. And he realized, with sudden unease, the kind of neighborhoods her projects would be in. He'd rather hoped never to return to them.

On the other hand the past he had been so certain he had left behind was reemerging, and he regarded his unease with some distaste. Houston Whitford was not a man who shirked.

Not from *knowing* eyes, not from the demons in his past.

He would face the pull of her and the desire to push away his past in the very same way—head-on. He was not running away from anything. There was nothing he could not handle for two short days.

"Okay," he said again. "Two days."

Maybe it was because it felt as if he'd made a concession and was giving her false hope—maybe it was to fight the light in her face—that he added, "But Prom Dreams is already gone. And in two days all my other decisions are final."

CHAPTER THREE

MOLLY was glad to be home. Today easily qualified as one of the worst of her life.

Right up there with the day her father had announced her parents' plan to divorce, right up there with the day she had come home from work to find her message machine blinking, Chuck's voice on the other end.

"Sorry, sweetheart, moving on. A great opportunity in Costa Rica."

Not even the courtesy of a face-to-face breakup. Of course, if he'd taken the time to do that, he might have jeopardized his chances of getting away with the contents, meager as they had been, of her bank account.

A note had arrived, postmarked from Costa Rica, promising to pay her back, and also telling her not to totally blame him. *Sweetheart, you're a pushover. Don't let the next guy get away with pushing you around*. To prove she was not a pushover, she had taken the note directly to the police and it had been added to her complaint against Chuck.

A kindly desk sergeant had told her not to hold her breath about them ever finding him or him ever sending a check. And he'd been right. So far, no checks, but the advice had probably been worth it, even if so far, there had been no *next* guy.

Besides, the emptied bank account had really been a small price to pay to be rid of Chuck, she thought, and then felt startled. It was the first time she had seen his defection in that light.

Was it Houston, with his hard-headed pragmatism, that was making her see things differently? Surely not! For all that he was a powerful presence, there was no way she could be evaluating Chuck through his eyes!

And finding the former coming up so lacking.

Perhaps change in general forced one to evaluate one's life in a different light?

For instance, she was suddenly glad she had

never given in to Chuck's pressure to move in with her, that she had clung to her traditional values, that it was marriage or nothing.

She had actually allowed Chuck access to her bank account to take the sting out of that decision, one she'd been unusually firm about even in the face of Chuck's irritation.

Because of that decision today she could feel grateful that her apartment remained a tiny, cozy space, all hers, no residue of Chuck here.

Usually her living room welcomed her, white slipcovers over two worn love seats that faced each other, fresh flowers in a vase on the coffee table between the sofas. The throw cushions were new to pick up the colors from her most prized possession, acquired since Chuck's defection from her life.

It was a large, expensively framed art poster of a flamboyantly colored hot air balloon rising at dawn over the golden mists of the Napa Valley.

There were two people standing at the side of the basket of the rising balloon, sharing the experience and each other at a deep level that the photographer had managed to capture. Tonight, Molly Michaels looked at it with the fresh eyes of one who had been judged, and felt defensive.

She told herself she hadn't bought it because she was a *romantic,* as a subliminal nod to all she still wanted to believe in. No, Molly had purchased the piece because it spoke to the human spirit's ability to rise above turmoil, to experience peace and beauty despite disappointments and betrayals.

And that's why she'd tried on the wedding dress, too?

The unwanted thoughts made her much loved living space feel like a frail refuge from the unexpected storm that was battering her world.

Hurricane Houston, she told herself, out loud trying for a wry careless note, but instead she found she had conjured an image of his eyes that threatened to invade even the coziness of her safe place.

Which just went to show that Houston Whitford was a man she *really* would have to defend herself against, if the mere remembering of the light in his eyes could make him have more presence here in her tiny sanctuary than Chuck had ever had.

That begged another question. If someone like Chuck—unwilling to accept responsibility for anything, including his theft of her bank account—could devastate her life so totally, how much more havoc could a more powerful man wreak on the life of the unwary?

Molly remembered the touch of Houston's hands on her neck, and shivered, remembering how hard the texture of his skin had been, a forewarning he was much tougher than the exquisite tailoring of the suit had prepared her for.

Have you ever been hungry?

What had she seen in him in that moment? Not with her eyes, really, her heart. Her heart had sensed something, known something about him that he did not want people to know.

Stop it, she ordered herself. She was only proving he was right. Hearts sensing something that the eyes could not see was romantic hogwash.

He had already axed Prom Dreams. That's what she needed to see! She was dealing with a man who was heartless!

Though she rarely drank and never during the week, she poured herself a glass of the Biale Black Chicken Zinfandel from the region depicted on the poster. She raised her glass to the rising hot air balloon.

"To dreams," she said, even though it was probably proving that Houston Whitford was right again. A romantic despite her efforts to cure herself of it. She amended her toast, lifted the wineglass to the photo again. "To hope."

With uncharacteristic uncertainty tormenting her, Molly spent the evening reviewing her projects—alternately defending each and every one, and then trying to decide which ones to take him to in the two days he had reluctantly allotted her.

And she tried desperately to think of a way to save Prom Dreams. They always had lots of donations of fine gowns, but never enough. It had to be supplemented for each girl who wanted a dress to get one. The thought of phoning the project coordinator and canceling it turned her stomach. Hearts would be broken! For months, girls looked forward to the night the Greenwich Village shop, Now and Zen, was transformed into prom dress heaven.

Could she wait? Hope for a change of heart on his part? A miracle?

If she could convince him of the merit of her other projects, would there be a chance he might develop faith in her abilities? Could she then convince him Prom Dreams had to be saved?

She was not used to having to prove herself at work! The supportive atmosphere at Second Chances had always been such that she felt respected, appreciated and approved of! None of her projects had ever come under fire, none had ever been dismissed as trivial! Of course there had been a few mistakes along the way, but no one had ever made her feel incompetent because of them! She had always been given the gift of implicit trust.

That was part of the *soul* of Second Chances. It trusted the best in everyone would come out if it was encouraged!

Could she make Houston Whitford see that soul as she had promised? Could she make him feel that sense of family he was so cynical about? Could she make him understand the importance of it in a world too cold, and too capitalistic and too focused on those precious bottom lines?

But she was suddenly very aware she did not want to think of Houston Whitford in the context of a family.

That felt as if it would be the most dangerous thing of all, as if it would confirm what her heart insisted it had glimpsed in him when he had talked about hunger and hardship.

That he was lonely. That never had a man needed a family more than he did.

Stop it, she told herself. That was exactly the kind of thinking that got her into trouble, made her a pushover as Chuck had so generously pointed out from the beaches of Costa Rica, no doubt while sipping Margaritas paid for with her money! Molly took far too long the next morning choosing her outfit, but she knew she needed to look and feel every inch a professional, on even footing, in a position to command both respect and straight answers.

She had to erase the message that the wedding dress had given. She had to be seen as a woman who knew her job, and was a capable and complete professional.

The suit Molly chose was perfect—Calvin Klein, one-inch-above-the-knee black skirt, tailored matching jacket over a sexy hot-pink camisole. But somehow it wasn't quite right, and she changed it.

"You don't have time for this," she wailed, and yet somehow *looking* calm and confident when that was the last thing she was feeling seemed more important than ever.

She ended up in a white blouse and a spring skirt—splashes of lime-green and lemon-yellow—that was decidedly flirty in its cut and movement. She undid an extra button on the blouse. Did it back up. Raced for the door.

She undid the top button again as she walk-ran the short distance to work. She was going to need every advantage she could call into play to work with that man! It seemed only fair that she should keep him as off balance as he made her.

Only as soon as she entered the office she could see they were not even playing in the same league when it came to the "off balance" department.

The Second Chances office as she had always known it was no more.

In its place was a construction zone. Sawhorses had been set up and a carpenter was measuring lengths of very expensive looking crown molding on them. One painter was putting down drop cloths, another was leaning on Tish the receptionist's desk, making her blush. An official looking man with a clipboard was peering into filing cabinets making notes. A series of blueprint drawings were out on the floor.

Molly had ordered herself to start differently today. To be a complete professional, no matter what.

Bursting into tears didn't seem to qualify!

How could he do this? He had promised to give her a chance to show him where funding was needed! How could he be tearing down the office without consulting the people who worked there? Without asking them what they needed and wanted? Why had she thought, from a momentary glimpse of something in his eyes, that he had a soft side? That she could trust him? Wasn't that the mistake she insisted on making over and over again?

Worst of all, Prom Dreams was the first of her many projects being axed for lack of funding, and Houston Whitford was in a redecorating frenzy? There were four complete strangers hard at work in the outer office, all of whom would be getting paid, and probably astronomical amounts! Molly could hear the sounds of more workers, a circular saw screaming in a back room.

Calm and control, Molly ordered herself. She curled her hands in her skirt to remind herself why she had taken such care choosing it. *To appear a total professional.*

Storming his office screaming could not possibly accomplish that. Not possibly.

Instead, she slid under an open ladder—defying the bad luck that could bring—and went through the door of her own office. Molly needed to gather her wits and hopefully to delay that temper—the unfortunate but well-deserved legacy she shared with other redheads—from progressing to a boil.

But try as she might, she could not stop the thoughts. *Office renovation? Instead of Prom Dreams?*

Houston Whitford had insinuated there was *no* money, not that he was reallocating the funds they had. She needed to gather herself, to figure out how to deal with this, how to put a stop to it before he'd spent all the money. Saving Prom Dreams was going to be the least of her problems if he kept this up. Everything would be gone!

A woman backed out of the closet, and Molly gave a startled squeak.

"Oh, so sorry to startle you. I'm the design consultant. I specialize in office space and you need storage solutions. I think we can go up, take advantage of the height of this room. And what do you think of ochre for a paint color? Iron not yellow?"

He'd told her there was no money for Prom Dreams, but there was apparently all kinds of money for things he considered a priority.

Foolish, stupid things, like construction and consultants, that could suck up a ton of money in the blink of an eye. How could complete strangers have any idea what was best for Second Chances?

Molly was suddenly so angry with herself for always believing the best of people, for always being the reasonable one, for always giving the benefit of the doubt.

Pushover, an imaginary Chuck toasted her with his Margarita.

She had to make a stand for the things she believed in. Be strong, and not so easy for people to take advantage of.

"The only colors I want to discuss are the colors of prom dresses," she told the surprised consultant.

Molly's heart was beating like a meek and mild schoolteacher about to do battle with a world-wise gunslinger. But it didn't matter to her that she was unarmed. She had her spirit!

She had her backbone! She turned on her heel, and strode toward the O.K. Corral at high noon.

This had already gone too far. She didn't want another penny spent! He had called her favorite program frivolous? How dare he!

She stopped at the threshold of Miss Viv's office, where Houston Whitford had set up shop.

He looked unreasonably gorgeous this morning. Better than a man had any right to look. "Ready to go?" he asked mildly, as if he wasn't tearing her whole world apart. "I need half an hour or so, and then I'm all yours."

Don't even be sidetracked by what a man like that being *all yours* could mean, she warned the part of herself that was all too ready to veer toward the romantic!

Molly took a deep breath and said firmly, not the least sidetracked, "This high-handed hijacking of Second Chances money is unacceptable to me."

He cocked his head at her as if he found her interesting, maybe even faintly amusing.

"Mr. Whitford, there is no nice way to say this. Miss Viv left you in charge for a reason I cannot even fathom, but she could not have been expecting this! This is a terrible waste of the resources Miss Viv has spent her life marshalling! Construction and consultants? Are you trying to break her heart? Her spirit?"

She was quite pleased with herself, assertive, a realist, speaking a language he could understand! Well, maybe the last two lines had veered just a touch toward the romantic.

Still, Molly was making it clear to herself and to him that she wasn't *trusting* anymore.

Not that he seemed to be taking her seriously!

"From what I've seen of Miss Viv," he said, with a touch of infuriating wryness, "it would take a little more than a new paint job, a wall or two coming down, to break her spirit."

"Are you deliberately missing my point? This is *not* what Second Chances is about. We are not about slick exteriors! We are about helping people, and being of genuine service to our community."

"Pretty hard to do if you go belly-up," he pointed out mildly.

"Isn't a renovation of this magnitude going to rush us toward that end?"

He actually smiled. "Not with me in charge, it isn't."

She stared at him, unnerved by the colossal arrogance of the man, his confidence in himself, by his absolute calm in the face of her confusion, as if ripping apart people's lives was all ho-hum to him!

"There's someone in my office wanting to know if I like ochre," Molly continued dangerously. "Not the yellow ochre, the iron one. I'd rather have new prom dresses."

"I thought I made it clear the prom dress issue was closed. As for design money for the offices, I've allocated that from a separate budget."

"I don't care what kind of shell game you play with the money! It's all coming from the same pot, isn't it?"

He didn't answer her. He was not even trying to disguise the fact, now, that he found her attempts at assertiveness amusing. She tried, desperately, to make him see reason.

"Girls who are dying to have a nice dress won't get one, but we'll have the poshest offices in the East Village! Doesn't something strike you as very wrong about that?"

But even as Molly said it, she was aware it wasn't all about the girls and their dresses. Maybe even most of it wasn't about that.

It was about turning over control. Or not turning over control. To people who had not proven themselves deserving. Especially handsome men people!

"Actually, no, it doesn't strike me as wrong. Prom dresses in the face of all this need is what's *wrong*."

Part of her said maybe her new boss was not the best place to start in standing her ground. On the other hand, maybe it was just time for her to learn to stand her ground no matter who it was with.

"This is what's wrong," she said. "How on earth can you possibly justify this extravagance? How? How can you march in here, knowing nothing about this organization, and start making these sweeping changes?"

"I've made it my business to know about the organization. The changes you're seeing today are largely cosmetic." A tiny smile touched his lips. "Sweeping is tomorrow."

"Don't mock me," she said. "You told me I could have two days to convince you what Second Chances really needs."

"I did. And I'm ready to go."

"But you're already spending all our money!"

"Second Chances hasn't begun to capitalize on the kind of money that's available to organizations like this. A charity, for all its noble purposes, is still a business. A business has to run efficiently, this kind of business has to make an impression. Every single person who walks through the front door of this office has the potential to be the person who could donate a million dollars to Second Chances. You have one chance to make a first impression, to capitalize on that opportunity. One. Trust me with this."

Molly suddenly felt like a wreck, her attempt

to be assertive backfiring and leaving her feeling regretful and uncertain. Trust him?

Good grief, was there a job she was worse at than choosing whom to trust? She wished Miss Viv was here to walk her through this minefield she found herself in—that she hated finding herself in! Second Chances was supposed to be the place where she didn't feel like this: threatened, as if your whole world could be whipped out from under you in the blink of an eye.

Molly, there are going to be some changes.

"I'll be ready in half an hour," she said with all the dignity she could muster. She was very aware that it rested on her shoulders to save the essence of Second Chances. If it was left to him the family feeling would be stripped from this place as ruthlessly as Vikings stripped treasures from the monasteries they were sacking!

The consultant, thankfully, was gone from her office, and Molly sat down at her desk, aware she was shaking from her heated encounter with Houston, and determined to try to act as if it was a normal day, to regain her equilibrium. She would open her e-mail first.

Resolutely she tapped her keyboard and her computer screen came up. She was relieved to see an e-mail from Miss Viv.

Please give me direction, she whispered to the computer. *Please show me how to handle this, how to save what is most important about us. The love.*

Aware she was holding her breath, Molly clicked. No message—a paperclip indicated an attachment.

She clicked on the paperclip and a video opened. It was a grainy picture of a gorgeous hot air balloon, its colors, purple, yellow, red, green, vibrant against a flawless blue sky, rising majestically into the air. What did this have to do with Miss Viv?

The utter beauty of the picture was in such sharp contrast to the ugly reality of the changes being wrought in her life that Molly felt tears prick her eyes. She had always thought a ride in a hot air balloon would be the most incredible experience *ever*. Just last night she had toasted this very vision.

She squinted at the picture, and it came into focus. Two little old ladies were waving enthusiastically from the basket of the balloon. One of them blew a kiss.

Molly frowned, squinted hard at the grainy picture and gasped.

What was Miss Viv doing living Molly's dream? If this video was any indication, Miss Viv had complete trust in Houston Whitford being left in charge! Apparently she wasn't giving her life back here—or her Second Chances family—a single second thought.

In fact, Miss Viv was waving with enthusiasm, decidedly carefree, apparently having the time of her life. It made Molly have the disloyal thought that maybe she, Molly, had allowed Second Chances to become too much to her.

Molly's job, her career, especially in the awful months since Chuck, had become her whole life, instead of just a part of it.

What had happened to her own dreams?

"Dreams are dangerous," she reminded herself.

But that didn't stop her from envying the carefree vision Miss Viv had sent her. She wished, fervently, that they could change places!

She hit the reply button to Miss Viv's e-mail. "Call home," she wrote. "Urgent!"

CHAPTER FOUR

HOUSTON regarded the empty place where Molly had just stood, berating him, with interest. In terms of the reins of this place being handed over to her one day, it was a good thing that she was willing to stand up for issues that were important to her. She had made her points clearly, and with no ultimatums, which he appreciated.

He would be unwilling to recommend her for the head spot if she was every bit as soft as she looked. But, no, she was willing to go to battle, to stand her ground.

Unreasonable as it was that she had chosen him to stand it with! And her emotional attachment to the dress thing was a con that clearly nullified the pro of her ability to stand up.

Unreasonable as it was that the fight in her had

made her just as attractive as her sweetness in that wedding dress yesterday.

Maybe more so. Fights he knew how to handle. Sweetness, that was something else.

Still, for as analytical as he was trying to be, he had to acknowledge he was just a little miffed. He had become accustomed to answering to no one, he had earned the unquestioning respect of his team and the companies he worked for.

When Precision Solutions went in, Houston Whitford's track record proved productivity went up. And revenue. Jobs were not lost as a result of his team's efforts, but gained. Companies were put on the road to health, revitalized, reenergized.

There was nothing personal about what he did: it purely played to his greatest strengths, his substantial analytical skills. Except for the satisfaction he took in being the best, there was no emotion attached to his work.

Unlike Molly Michaels, most people appreciated that. They appreciated his approach, how fast he did things, how real and remarkable the changes he brought were. When he said cut something, it was cut, no questions asked.

No arguments!

They *thanked* him for the teams of experts, the new computers and ergonomically designed offices, and carefully researched paint colors that aided higher productivity.

"Maybe she'll thank you someday," he told himself, and then laughed at the unlikelihood of that scenario, and also at himself, for somehow wanting her approval.

This would teach him to deny his instincts. He had known not to tackle the charity. He had known he was going to come up against obstacles in the casually run establishment that he would never come across in the business world.

A redheaded vixen calling him down and questioning his judgment being a case in point!

But how could he have refused this? How could he refuse Beebee—or her circle of friends—anything? He owed his life to her, and to them. In those frightening days after his father had first been arrested, and his mother had quickly defected with another man—Houston had been making the disastrous mistake of trying to mask his fear with the anger that came so much more easily in his family.

He'd already worked his way through two foster homes when suddenly there had been Beebee. He had been in a destructive mode and had thrown a rock through the window of her car, parked on a dark street.

She had caught him red-handed, stunned him by not being the least afraid of him. Instead, she had looked at him with that same terrible *knowing* in her eyes that he had glimpsed in Molly's eyes yesterday.

And she had taken a chance. Recently widowed, and recently retired as a court judge, she had been looking for something to fill the sudden emptiness of her days. He still was not quite sure what twist of fate had made that *something* him.

And a world had opened up to him that had always been closed before. A world of wealth and privilege, yes, but more, a world without aggression, without things breaking in the night, without hunger, without harsh words.

It was also a world where things were expected of him that had never been required before.

Hard work. Honesty. Decency. She had gathered her friends, her family, her circle—including Miss Viv—around him. Teaching him the tools for surviving and flourishing in a different kind of world.

Houston shook his head, trying to clear away those memories, knowing they would not help him remain detached and analytical in his current circumstances.

Houston was also aware that it was a careful balancing act he needed to do. He needed to save the charity of the women who had saved him. He needed to decipher whether Molly was worthy to take the helm, but he could not afford to alienate her in the process, even if in some way, alienating her would make him feel safer.

It was more than evident to him, after plowing his way through Miss Viv's chaotic paperwork, that Molly Michaels was practically running the whole show here. Would she do better at that if she was performing in an official capacity? Or worse? That was one of the things he needed to know, absolutely, before Miss Viv came back.

He decided delay was not the better part of valor. He didn't want to allow Molly enough time to paint herself into a corner she could not get out of.

He went down the hallway to Molly's office. A ladder blocked the door; he surprised himself, because he was not superstitious, by stepping around it, rather than under it.

She was bent over her computer, her tongue caught between her teeth, a furious expression of concentration on her face.

She hit the send button on something, spun her chair around to face him, her arms folded over her chest.

"I'm hoping," he said, "that you'll give the changes here the same kind of chance to prove their merit that I'm giving you to prove the merit of your programs."

"Except Prom Dreams," she reminded him sourly.

"Except that," he agreed with absolutely no regret. "Let's give each other a chance."

She looked like she was all done giving people chances, residue from her *cad,* and the new wound, the loss of Prom Dreams.

And yet he could see from the look on her face that she was basically undamaged by life. Willing to believe. Wanting to trust. A *romantic* whether she wanted to believe it of herself or not.

Houston Whitford did not know if he was the person to be trusted with all that goodness, all that softness, all that compassion. He didn't know if the future of Second Chances could be trusted with it, either.

"All right," she said, but doubtfully.

"Great. Where are we going first?"

"I want to show you a garden project we've developed."

Funny, that was exactly what he wanted to see. And probably not for the reason Molly hoped, either. That land was listed as one of Second Chance's assets.

He handed her a camera. "Take lots of pictures today. I can use them for fundraising promotional brochures."

The garden project would be such a good way to show Houston what Second Chances *really* did.

As they arrived it was evident spring cleanup was going on today. About a dozen rake and shovel wielding volunteers were in the tiny lot, a haven of green sandwiched between two dilapidated old buildings. Most of the people there were old, at least retirement age. But the reality of the neighborhood was reflected in the fact many of them had children with them, grandchildren that they cared for.

"This plot used to be a terrible eyesore on this block," Molly told Houston. "Look at it now."

He only nodded, seeming distant, uncharmed by the sprouting plants, the fresh turned soil, the new bedding plants, the enthusiasm of the volunteers.

Molly shook her head, exasperated with him, and then turned her back on him. She was greeted warmly, soon at the center of hugs.

She felt at the heart of things. Mrs. Zarkonsky would be getting her hip replacement soon. Mrs. Brant had a new grandson. Sly looks were being sent toward Mr. Smith and Mrs. Lane, a widower and a widow who were holding hands.

And then she saw Mary Bedford. She hadn't seen her since they had put the garden to bed in the fall. She'd had some bad news then about a grandson who had been serving overseas.

Molly went to her, took those frail hands in her own.

"How is your grandson?" she asked. "Riley, wasn't it?"

A tear slipped down a weathered cheek. "He didn't make it."

"Oh, Mary, I'm so sorry."

"Please don't be sorry."

"How can I not be? He was so young!"

Mary reached up and rested a weathered hand against her cheek. It reminded Molly of being with Miss Viv when she looked into those eyes that were so fierce with love.

"He may have been young," she said, "but he lived every single day to the fullest. There are people my age who cannot say that. Not even close."

"That is true," Molly said.

"And he was like you, Molly."

"Like me?" she said, startled at being compared to the young hero.

"For so many of your generation it seems to be all about *things*. Bank accounts, and stuff, telephones stuck in your ears. But for Riley, it was about being of service. About helping other people. And that's what it's about for you, too."

Molly remembered sending that message to Miss Viv this morning, pleading for direction.

And here was her answer, as if you could not send out a plea for direction like the one she had sent without an answer coming from somewhere.

Ever since the crushing end of her relationship with Chuck, Molly had questioned everything about herself, had a terrible sense that she approached life all wrong.

And now she saw that wasn't true at all. She was not going to lose what was best about herself because she'd been hurt.

And then she became aware of her new boss watching her, a cynical look on his face.

For a moment she criticized herself, was tempted to see herself through his eyes. I *am too soft,* she thought. *He sees it.* For a moment she reminded herself of her vow, since Chuck, to be something else.

But then she realized that since Chuck she *had* become something else: unsure, resentful, self-pitying, bitter, frightened.

When life took a run at you, she wondered, did it chip away at who you were, or did it solidify who you really were? Maybe that was what she had missed: it was her *choice.*

"The days of all our lives are short," Mary said, and patted her on the arm. "Don't waste any of it."

Don't waste any of it, Molly thought, being frightened instead of brave, playing it safe instead of giving it the gift of who you really were.

The sun was so warm on her uplifted face, and she could feel the softness of Mrs. Bedford's tiny, frail hand in hers. And she could also feel the hope and strength in it.

Molly could feel love.

And if she allowed what Chuck—what life— had done to her to take that from her, to make her as cynical as the man watching her, then hadn't she lost the most important thing of all?

Herself.

She was what she was. If that meant she was going to get hurt from time to time, wasn't that so much better than the alternative?

She glanced again at Houston. That was the alternative. To be so closed to these small miracles. To know the price of everything and the value of nothing.

She suddenly felt sorry for him, standing there, aloof. His clothing and his car, even the way he stood, said he was so successful.

But he was alone, in amongst all the wonder

of the morning, and these people reaching out to each other in love, he was alone.

And maybe that was none of her business, and maybe she could get badly hurt trying to show him there was something else, but Molly suddenly knew she could not show him the soul of Second Chances unless she was willing to show him her own.

And it wasn't closed and guarded.

When she had put on that wedding dress yesterday for some reason she had felt more herself than she had felt in a long time.

Hope filled. A believer in goodness and dreams. Someone who trusted the future. Someone with something to give.

Love.

The word came to her again, filled her. She was not sure she wanted to be thinking of a word like that in such close proximity to a man like him, and if she had not just decided to be brave she might not have. She might have turned her back on him, and gone back to the caring that waited to encircle her.

But he needed it more than she did.

"Houston," she said, and waved him over. "Come meet Mary."

He came into the circle, reluctantly. And then Mary had her arms around his neck and was hugging him hard, and even as he tried to disentangle himself, Molly saw something flicker in his face, and smiled to herself.

She was pretty sure she had just seen his soul, too. And it wasn't nearly as hard-nosed as he wanted everyone to believe.

The sun was warm on the lot and she was given a tray of bedding plants and a small hand spade. Soon she was on her knees between Mrs. Zarkonsky and Mr. Philly. Mrs. Zarkonsky eyed Houston appreciatively and handed him a shovel. "You," she said. "Young. Strong. Work."

"Oh, no," Molly said, starting to brush off her knees and get up. "He's…" She was going to say *not dressed for it,* but then neither was she, and it hadn't stopped her.

He held up a hand before she could get to her feet, let her know that would be the day that she would have to *defend* him, and followed the old woman who soon had him shoveling dirt as if he was a farm laborer.

Molly glanced over from time to time. The jacket came off. The sleeves were rolled up. Sweat beaded on his forehead. Was it that moment of recognizing who she really was that made her feel so vulnerable watching him? That made her recognize she was weak and he was strong, she was soft and he was hard? The world yearned for balance, maybe that was why men and women yearned for each other even in the face of that yearning being a hazardous endeavor.

Houston put his back into it, all mouthwatering masculine grace and strength. Molly remembered the camera, had an excuse to focus on him.

Probably a mistake. He was gloriously and completely male as he tackled that pile of dirt.

"He looks like a nice boy," Mary said, following her gaze, but then whispered, "but a little snobby, I think."

Molly laughed. Yes, he was. Or at least that was what he wanted people to believe. That he

was untouchable. That he was not a part of what
they were a part of. Somewhere in there, she
could see it on his face he was just a nice boy,
who wanted to belong, but who was holding
something back in himself.

Was she reading too much into him?

Probably, but that's who she was, and that's
what she did. She rescued strays. Funny she
would see that in him, the man who held himself with such confidence, but she did.

Because that's what she did. She saw the best
in people. And she wasn't going to change because it had hurt her.

She was going to be stronger than that.

Molly was no more dressed for this kind of
work than Houston. But she went and got a
spade and began to shift the same pile of topsoil
he was working on. What better way to show
him *soul* than people willing to work so hard
for what they wanted? The spirit of community
was sprouting in the garden with as much vitality as the plants.

The spring sun shone brightly, somewhere
a bird sang. What could be better than this,

working side by side, to create an oasis of green in the middle of the busy city? There was magic here. It was in the sights and the sounds, in the smell of the fresh earth.

Of course, his smell was in her nostrils, too, tangy and clean. And there was something about the way a bead of sweat slipped down his temple that made her breath catch in her throat.

Romantic weakness, she warned herself, but halfheartedly. Why not just enjoy this moment, the fact it included the masculine beauty of him? Now, if only he could join in, instead of be apart. There was a look on his face that was focused but remote, as if he was immune to the magic of the day.

Oh, well, that was his problem. She was going to enjoy her day, especially with this new sense of having discovered who she was.

She gave herself over to the task at hand, placed her shovel, then jumped on it with both feet to drive it in to the dirt. It was probably because he was watching—or maybe because of the desperately unsuited shoes—that things went sideways. The shovel fell to one side, throwing her against him.

His arm closed around her in reaction. She felt the hardness of his palm tingling on the sensitive upper skin of her arm. The intoxicating scent of him intensified. He held her arm just a beat longer than he had to, and she felt the seductive and exhilarating *zing* of pure chemistry.

When he had touched her yesterday, she had felt these things, but he had looked only remote. Today, she saw something pulse through his eyes, charged, before it was quickly doused and he let go of her arm.

Was it because she had made a decision to be who she really was that she couldn't resist playing with that *zing?* Or was it because she was powerless not to explore it, just a little?

"You're going to hurt yourself," he said with a rueful shake of his head. And then just in case she thought he had a weak place somewhere in him, that he might actually care, that he might be feeling something as intoxicatingly unprofessional as she was, he said, "Second Chances can't afford a compensation claim."

She smiled to herself, went back to shoveling.

He seemed just a little too pleased with himself.

She tossed a little dirt on his shoes.

"Hey," he warned her.

"Sorry," she said, insincerely. She tossed a little more.

He stopped, glared at her over the top of his shovel. She pretended it had been purely an accident, focused intently on her own shovel, her own dirt. He went back to work. She tossed a shovel full of dirt right on his shoes.

"Hey!" he said, extricating his feet.

"Watch where you put your feet," she said solemnly. "Second Chances can't afford to buy you new shoes."

She giggled, and shoveled, but she knew he was regarding her over the top of his shovel, and when she glanced at him, some of that remoteness had gone from his eyes, *finally,* and this time it didn't come back. He went back to work.

Plop. Dirt on his shoes.

"Would you stop it?" he said.

"Stop what?" she asked innocently.

"You have something against my shoes?"

"No, they're very nice shoes."

"I know how to make you behave," he whispered.

She laughed. This is what she had wanted. To know if there was something in him that was playful, a place she could *reach*. "No, you don't."

He dangled it in front of her eyes.

A worm! She took a step back from him. "Houston! That's not funny!" But, darn it, in a way it was.

"What's not funny?" he said. "Throwing dirt on people's shoes?"

"I hate worms. Does our compensation package cover hysteria?"

"You would get hysterical if I, say, put this worm down your shirt?"

He sounded just a little too enthused about

that. It occurred to her they were flirting with each other, cautiously stepping around that little *zing,* looking at it from different angles, exploring it.

"No," she said, but he grinned wickedly, sensing the lie.

The grin changed everything about him. Everything. He went from being too uptight and too professional to being a carefree young man, covered in dirt and sweat, real and human.

It seemed to her taking that chance on showing him who she really was was paying off somehow.

Until he did a practice lunge toward her with the worm. Because she really did hate worms!

"If I tell your girlfriend you were holding worms with your bare hands today, she may never hold your hand again."

"I don't have a girlfriend."

Ah, it was a weakness. She'd been fishing. But that's what worms were for!

He lunged at her again, the worm wiggled between his fingers. He looked devilishly happy when she squealed.

Then, as if he caught himself in the sin of having fun, he abruptly dropped the worm, went back to work.

She hesitated. It was probably a good time to follow his lead and back off. But, oh, to see him smile had changed something in her. Made her willing to take a risk. With a sigh of surrender, she tossed a shovel of dirt on his shoes. And he picked up that worm.

"I warned you," he said.

"You'd have to catch me first!"

Molly threw down her shovel and ran. He came right after her, she could hear his footfalls and his breathing. She glanced over her shoulder and saw he was chasing her, holding out the worm. She gave a little snicker, and put on a burst of speed. At one point, she was sure that horrible worm actually touched her neck, and she shrieked, heard his rumble of breathless laughter, ran harder.

She managed to put a wheelbarrow full of plants between them. She turned and faced him. "Be reasonable," she pleaded breathlessly.

"The time for reason is done," he told her

sternly, but then that grin lit his face—boyish, devil-may-care, and he leaped the wheelbarrow with ease and the chase was back on.

The old people watched them indulgently as they chased through the garden. Finally the shoes betrayed her, and she went flying. She landed in a pile of soft but foul-smelling peat moss. He was immediately contrite. He dropped the worm and held out his hand—which she took with not a bit of hesitation. He pulled her to her feet with the same easy strength that he had shoveled with. Where did a man who crunched numbers get that kind of strength from? She had that feeling again, of something about him not adding up, but it was chased away by his laughter.

"You don't laugh enough," she said.

"How do you know?"

"I'm not sure. I just do. You are way too serious, aren't you?"

He held both her hands for a moment, reached out and touched a curl, brushed it back from out of her eyes.

"Maybe I am," he admitted.

Something in her felt absolutely weak with what she wanted at that moment. To make him laugh, but more, to *explore* all the reasons he didn't. To find out what, exactly, about him did not add up.

"Truce?" he said.

"Of course," she panted. She meant for all of it, their different views of Second Chances. All of it.

He reached over, snared the camera out of her pocket and took a picture of her.

"Don't," she protested. She could feel her hair falling out, she was pretty sure there was a smudge of dirt on her cheek, and probably on her derriere, too!

But naturally he didn't listen and so she stuck out her tongue at him and then struck a pose for him, and then called over some of the other gardeners. Arms over each other's shoulders, they performed an impromptu can-can for the camera before it all fell apart, everyone dissolving into laughter.

Houston smiled, but that moment of spontaneity was fading. Molly was aware that he saw that moment of playfulness differently to her. Possibly as a failing. Because he was still faintly removing himself from them. She had been welcomed into the folds of the group, he stood outside it.

Lonely, she thought. *There was something so lonely about him.* And she felt that feeling, again, of wanting to explore.

And maybe to save. Just like she saved her strays. But somehow, looking at the handsome, remote cast of his face, she knew he would hate it that she had seen anything in him that needed saving. That *needed,* period.

They got back in the car, she waved to the old people. Molly was aware she was thrilled with how the morning had gone, by its unexpected surprises, and especially how he had unexpectedly revealed something of himself.

"How are your hands?" she asked him. He held one out to her. An hour on a shovel had done nothing to that hand.

"I would have thought you would have blisters," she said.

"No, my hands are really tough."

"From?"

"I box."

"As in fight?"

He laughed. "Not really. It's more the workout I like."

So, her suspicions that he was not quite who he said were unfounded. He was a high-powered businessman who sought fitness at a high-powered level.

That showed in every beautiful, mesmerizing male inch of him!

"Wasn't that a wonderful morning?" she asked, trying to solidify the camaraderie that had blossomed so briefly between them. "I promised I would show you the soul of Second Chances and that's part of it! What a lovely sense of community, of reclaiming that lot, of bringing something beautiful to a place where there was ugliness."

She became aware he was staring straight ahead. Her feeling of deflation was immediate. "You didn't feel it?"

"Molly, it's a nice project. The warm and fuzzy feel good kind."

She heard the *but* in his voice, sensed it in the set of his shoulders. Naturally he would be immune to warm fuzzy feeling good.

"But it's my job to ask if it makes good economic sense. Second Chances owns that lot, correct?"

She nodded reluctantly. Good economic sense after the magical hour they had just spent? "It was donated to us. Years ago. Before I came on board it was just an empty lot that no one did anything with."

If she was expecting congratulations on her innovative thought she was sadly disappointed!

"Were there provisos on the donation?"

"Not that I know of."

"I'll have to do some homework."

"But why?"

"I have to ask these questions. Is that the best use of that lot? It provides a green space, about a dozen people seem to actually enjoy it. Could it be liquidated and the capital used to help more people? Could it be developed—a parking lot or a commercial building—providing a stream of income into perpetuity? Providing jobs and income for the neighborhood?"

"A parking lot?" she gasped. And then she saw *exactly* what he was doing. Distancing himself from the morning they had just shared—distancing himself from the satisfaction of hard work and the joy of laughter and the admiration of people who would love him.

Distancing himself from her. Did he know she had *seen* him? Did he suspect she had uncovered things about him he kept hidden?

He didn't like *feelings*. She should know that firsthand. Chuck had had a way of rolling his eyes when she had asked him how he was feeling that had made her stop asking!

But, naive as it might be, she was pretty sure she had just glimpsed the real Houston Whitford, something shining under those layers of defenses.

And she wasn't quite ready to let that go. It didn't have to be personal. No, she could make it a mission, for the good of Second Chances, she told herself, she would get past all those defenses.

For the good of Second Chances she was going to rescue him from his lonely world.

CHAPTER FIVE

"Hey," she said, "there's Now and Zen."

She could clearly see he was disappointed that she had not risen to the bait of him saying he was going to build a parking lot over the garden project.

"Why don't we go in?" she suggested. "You can look for some gardening shoes."

She was not going to give up on him. He was not as hard-nosed as he wanted to seem. She just knew it.

How could he spend a morning like they had just spent in the loveliness of that garden, and want to put up a parking lot? Giving up wasn't in her nature. She was finding a way to shake him up, to make him see, to make him connect! Lighten him up.

And Now and Zen was just plain fun.

"Would you like to stop and have a look?"

He shrugged, regarded her thoughtfully as if he suspected she was up to something but just wasn't quite sure what. "Why not?"

Possibly another mistake, she thought as they went in the door to the delightful dimness and clutter of Now and Zen. He'd probably be crunching the numbers on this place, too. Figuring out if its magic could be bottled and sold, or repackaged and sold, or destroyed for profit.

Stop it, she ordered herself. *Show him. Invite him into this world. He's lonely. He has to be in his uptight little world where everything has a price and nothing has value.*

She tried to remind herself there was a risk of getting hurt in performing a rescue of this nature, but it was a sacrifice she was making for Second Chances! Second Chances needed for him to be the better man that she was sure she saw in there somewhere, sure she had seen when he was putting his all into that shovel.

That was muscle, a cynical voice cautioned her, *not a sign of a better man.*

Something caught her eye. She took a deep

breath, plucked the black cowboy hat from the rack and held it out to him in one last attempt to get him to come into her world, to see it all through her eyes.

"Here, try this on."

Now and Zen was not like the other stores, but funky, laid-back, a place that encouraged the bohemian.

The whole atmosphere in the store said, *Have fun!*

He looked at her, shook his head, she thought in refusal. But then he said, "If I try that on, I get to pick something for you to try on."

She felt the thrill of his surrender. So, formidable as his discipline was, she could entice him to play with her!

"That's not fair," Molly said. "You can clearly see what I want you to try on, but you're asking me for carte blanche. I mean you could pick a bikini!"

"Did you see one?" he asked with such unabashed hopefulness that she laughed. It confirmed he did have a playful side. And she fully intended to coax it to the surface, even if she had to wear a bikini to do it.

Besides, the temptation to see him in the hat—as the gunslinger—proved too great to resist, even at the risk that he might turn up a bikini!

"Okay," she said. "If you try this on, I'll try something on that you pick."

"Anything?" He grinned wickedly.

There was that grin again, without defenses, the kind of smile that could melt a heart.

And show a woman a soul.

He took the hat from her.

"Anything," she said. The word took on new meaning as he set the hat on his head. It didn't look corny, it didn't even look like he was play-ing dress-up. He adjusted it, pulled the brim low over his brow. His eyes were shaded, sexy, silver.

She felt her mouth go dry. *Anything.* She had known that something else lurked between that oh so confident and composed exterior. Something dangerous. Something completely untamed. Could those things coexist with the better man that she was determined to see?

Or maybe what was dangerous and untamed was in her. In every woman, somewhere. Something that made a prim schoolteacher say to an outlaw, *anything. Anywhere.*

"My turn," he said, and disappeared down the rows. While he looked she looked some more, too. And came up with a black leather vest.

He appeared at her side, a hanger in his hand.

A feather boa dangled from it, an impossible and exotic blend of colors.

"There's Baldy's missing feathers!" she exclaimed.

"Baldy?"

"My budgie. With hardly any feathers. His name is Baldy." It was small talk. Nothing more. Why did it feel as if she was opening up her personal life, her world, to him?

"What happened to his feathers?"

"Stolen to make a boa. Kidding." She flung the boa dramatically around her neck. "I don't know what happened to his feathers. He was like that when I got him. If I didn't take him…" She slid her finger dramatically over her throat.

"You saved him," he said softly, but there was suspicion in his eyes, worthy of a gunslinger, *don't even think it about me.*

No sense letting on she already was!

"It was worth it. He's truly a hilarious little character, full of personality. People would be amazed by how loving he is."

This could only happen to her: standing in the middle of a crazy store, a boa around her neck, discussing a bald budgie with a glorious man with eyes that saw something about her that it felt like no one had ever seen before.

And somehow the word *love* had slipped into the conversation.

Molly took the boa in her hand and spun the long tail of it, deliberately moving away from a moment that was somehow too intense, more real than what she was ready for.

He stood back, studied her, nodded his approval. "You could wear it to work," he decided, taking the hint that something too intense—though delightful—had just passed between them.

"Depending where I worked!"

"Hey, if you can wear a wedding gown, you can wear that."

"I think not. Second Chances is all about image now!"

"Are you saying that in a good way?"

"Don't take it as I'm backing down on Prom Dreams, but yes, I suppose I could warm to the bigger picture at the office. Don't get bigheaded about it."

"It's just the hat that's making you make comments about my head size. I know it."

She handed him the vest. "This goes with it."

"Uh-uh," he said. "No freebies. If I try on something else, I get to pick something else for you."

"You didn't bring me a bikini, so I'll try to trust you."

"I couldn't find one, but I'll keep looking."

He slipped on the vest. She drew in her breath at the picture he was forming. Rather than looking funny, he looked coolly remote, as if he was stepping back in time, a man who could handle himself in difficult circumstances, who would step toward difficulty rather than away.

He turned away from her, went searching again, came back just as she was pulling faded jeans from a hanger.

He had a huge pair of pink glass clip-on earrings.

"Those look like chandeliers. Besides, pink looks terrible with my hair."

"Ah, well, I'm not that fond of what the hat is doing to mine, either."

She handed him the jeans.

"You're asking for it, lady. That means I have one more choice, too."

"You can't do any worse than these earrings! My ears are growing by the second."

His eyes fastened on her ears. For a moment it felt as if the air went out of the room. He hadn't touched her. He hadn't even leaned closer. How could she possibly have felt the heat of his lips on the tender flesh of her earlobe?

He spun away, headed across the store for one of the change rooms. She saw him stop and speak to Peggy for a moment, and then he disappeared into a change room.

Moments later, Peggy approached her with something. She held it out to Molly, reverently, across two arms. "He said he picks this," she said, wide-eyed, and then in a lower tone, "that man is hotter than Hades, Molly."

Peggy put her in the change room beside his. The dress fit her like a snakeskin. It dipped so low in the front V and an equally astonishing one at the back, that she had to take it off, remove her shoes and her underwear to do the dress justice. She put it back on and the lines between where she ended and the dress began were erased.

Now, that spectacular dress did her justice. It looked, not as if she was in a funky secondhand store, but ready to walk the red carpet. Molly recognized the intense over-the-top sensuality of the dress and tried to hide it by putting the feather boa back on.

It didn't work.

She peeked out of the dressing room, suddenly shy.

"All the way out," he said. He was standing there in his jeans and vest and hat, looking as dangerous as a gunslinger at high noon.

She stepped out, faked a confidence she wasn't feeling by setting a hand on the hip she cocked at him and flinging the boa over her shoulder.

His eyes widened.

She liked the look in them so much she turned around and let him see the dipping back V of the dress, that ended sinfully just short of showing her own dimples.

She glanced over her shoulder to see his reaction.

She tried to duck back into the change room, but his hand fell, with exquisite strength, on her shoulder. She froze and then turned slowly to face him.

"I do declare, miss, I thought you were a schoolmarm," he drawled, obviously playing with the outfit she had him in. Isn't this what she'd wanted? To get the walls down? To find the playful side of him? For them to connect?

But if his words were playful, the light in his eyes was anything but. How could he do this? How could he act as if he'd had a front row seat to her secret fantasy about him all the time? Well, she'd asked for it by handing him that hat!

"And I thought you were just an ordinary country gentleman," she cooed, playing along, *loving* this more than a woman should. "But you're not, are you?"

He cocked his head at her.

"An outlaw," she whispered. *Stealing unsuspecting hearts.*

She saw the barest of flinches when she said that, as if she had struck a nerve, as if there was something real in this little game they were playing. She was aware that he was backing away from her, not physically, but the smooth curtain coming down over his amazing eyes.

Again she had a sense, a niggle of a feeling, *there is something about this man that he does not want you to know.*

She was aware she should pay attention to that feeling.

One of the girls turned up the music that played over the store's system. It was not classical, something raunchy and offbeat, so instead of paying attention to that feeling, Molly wanted to lift her hands over her head and sway to it, invite him deeper into the game.

"Would you care to dance?" she asked, not wanting him to back away, not wanting that at all, not really caring who he was, but wanting to be who she really was, finally. Unafraid. Molly held her breath, waiting for his answer.

For a long moment—forever, while her heart stopped beating—he stood there, frozen to the spot. His struggle was clear in his eyes. He knew it wasn't professional. He knew they were crossing some line. He knew they were dancing with danger.

Then slowly, he held up his right hand in a gesture that could have been equally surrender or an invitation to put her hand there, in his.

She read it as invitation. Even though this wasn't the kind of dancing she meant, she stepped into him, slid her hand up to his. They stood there for a suspended moment, absolutely still, palm to palm. His eyes on her eyes, his breath stirring her hair. She could see his pulse beating in the hollow of his throat, she could smell his fragrance.

Then his fingers closed around hers. He rested his other hand lightly on her waist, missing the naked expanse of her back by a mere finger's width.

"The pleasure is all mine," he said. But he did not pull her closer. Instead, a stiffly formal schoolboy, ignoring the raunchy beat of the music, he danced her down the aisle of Now and Zen.

She didn't know how he managed not to hit anything in those claustrophobic aisles, because his eyes never left her face. They drank her in, as if he was memorizing her, as if he really was an outlaw, who would go away someday and could not promise he would come back.

Molly drank in the moment, savored it. The scent of him filling her nostrils, the exquisite touch of his hand on her back, the softness in his eyes as he looked down at her. She had intended to find out something about him, to nurse something about him to the surface.

Somehow her discoveries were about herself.

That she *longed* for this. To be touched. To be seen. To feel so exquisitely feminine. And cherished. To feel as if she was a mystery that someone desperately wanted to solve.

Ridiculous. They were virtually strangers. And he was her boss.

The song ended. Peggy and the other clerk applauded. His hands dropped away, and he stepped back from her. But his gaze held.

And for a moment, in his eyes, her other secret longings were revealed to Molly: babies crawling on the floor; a little boy in soccer; a young girl getting ready for prom, her father looking at her with those stern eyes, saying, *You are not wearing that.*

Molly had never had these kinds of thoughts with Chuck. She had dreamed of a wedding, yes, in detail she now saw had been excessive. A marriage? No. A vision of the future with Chuck had always eluded her.

Maybe because she had never really known what that future could feel like. Nothing in her chaotic family had given her the kind of hope she had just felt dancing down a crowded clothing aisle.

Hope for a world that tingled with liveliness, where the smallest of discoveries held the kernels of adventure, the promise that exploring another person was like exploring a strange country: exotic, full of unexpected pleasures and surprises. Beckoning. For the first time since Molly had split from Chuck she felt grateful. Not just a little bit grateful. Exceedingly.

She could have missed *this*. This single, electrifying moment of knowing.

Knowing there were things on this earth so wonderful they were beyond imagining. Knowing that there was something to this word called *love* that was more magnificent than any poem or song or piece of film had ever captured.

Love?

That word again in the space of a few minutes, not in the relatively safe context of a bald budgie this time, either.

Pull away from him, she ordered herself. He was casting a spell on her. She was forgetting she'd been hurt. She was forgetting the cynicism her childhood should have filled her with.

She was embracing the her she had glimpsed in the garden, who thought hope was a good thing.

But couldn't hope be the most dangerous thing of all?

Pull back, she ordered herself. *Molly, I mean it!* This wasn't what she had expected when she had decided to live a little more dangerously.

This was *a lot* more dangerously.

Yes, she had decided she needed to be true to herself, but this place she was going to now was a part of herself unexplored.

He was her boss, she told herself. In her eagerness to reach him, to draw him into the warmth of her world, she had crossed some line.

How did you get back to normal after something like that?

How did you go back to the office after that?

How did you keep your head? How did you not be a complete pushover?

"Dior," Peggy whispered, interrupting her thoughts. "I've been saving that dress for Prom Dreams. Do you want to see the poster I'm sending out to the schools to advertise the Prom Dreams evening? It just came in."

Molly slid Houston a look. Whatever softening had happened a moment ago was gone. He was watching her, coolly waiting for her to do what she needed to do.

But she couldn't.

The mention of the probably defunct Prom Dreams should have helped Molly rally her badly sagging defenses, make her forget this nonsense about bringing him out of his lonely world, showing him the meaning of soul.

It was just too dangerous a game she was playing.

On the other hand, she could probably trust him to do what she could not! To herd things back over the line to proper, to put up the walls between them.

* * *

Outside he said to her, no doubt about who was the boss now, "Why didn't you tell her Prom Dreams has been canceled?"

He said it coolly, the remoteness back in his eyes.

She recognized this was his pattern. Show something of himself, appeal to his emotion, like at the garden, and then he would back away from it. There he had tried to hide behind the threat of a parking lot.

This time by bringing up the sore point of Prom Dreams.

He knew, just as she did, that it was safer for them to argue than to chase each other with worms, to dance down dusty aisles.

But despite the fact she knew she should balance caution with this newly awakened sense of adventure, she felt unusually brave, as if she never had to play it safe again. Of course, the formidable obstacle of his will was probably going to keep her very safe whether she wanted to be or not!

She tilted her chin at him. "Why didn't you?"

"I guess I wanted to see if you could do it."

"I can. I will if I have to. But not yet. I'm hoping for a miracle," she admitted. Because that was who she was. A girl who could look at herself in a wedding dress, even after her own dreams had been shattered, even in the face of much evidence to the contrary, a girl who could still hope for the best, hope for the miracle of love to fix everything.

And for a moment, when his guard had gone down, dancing with him, she had believed maybe she would get her miracle after all....

"A miracle," he said with a sad shake of his head. He went and opened the car door for her, and drove back to Second Chances in silence as if somehow she had disappointed him and not the other way around.

A miracle, he thought. If people could really call down such a thing, surely they would not waste that power on a prom dress. Cure world hunger. Or cancer. He was annoyed at Molly.

For not doing as he had asked her—a thinly veiled order really—and canceling Prom

Dreams, at least she should have told that girl to get ready for the cancellation of it.

But more, for wheedling past his defenses. He had better things to be doing than dancing with her in a shabby store in Greenwich Village.

It was the type of experience that might make a man who knew better hope for a miracle.

But hadn't he hoped for that once?

The memory leaped over a wall that seemed to have chinks out of it that it had not had yesterday.

It was his birthday. He was about to turn fifteen. He'd been at Beebee's for months. He was living a life he could never have even dreamed for himself.

He had his own room. He had his own TV. He had his own bathroom. He had nice clothes.

And the miracle he was praying for was for his mother to call. Under that grand four-poster bed was a plain plastic bag, with everything he had owned when he came here packed in it.

Ready to go. In case his mother called. And wanted him back.

That was the miracle he had prayed for that had never come.

"I don't believe in miracles," he said to Molly, probably way more curtly than was necessary.

"That's too bad," she said sympathetically, forgiving his curtness, missing his point entirely that there was no room in the business world for dreamers. "That's really too bad.

"Why don't we call it a day?" she said brightly. "Tomorrow I'll take you to Sunshine and Lollipops, our preschool program. It's designed to assist working poor mothers, most of them single parents."

Houston Whitford contemplated that. Despite the professionalism of her delivery, he knew darn well what she was up to. She was taking down the bricks around his carefully compartmentalized world. She was *getting* to him. And she knew it. She knew it after he had chased her in the garden with that worm, danced with her.

She was having quite an impact on his legendary discipline and now she was going to try to hit him in his emotional epicenter to get her programs approved. Who could resist preschoolers, after all?

Me, he thought. She was going to try to win him over to her point of view by going for the heart instead of the head. It was very much the romantic versus the realist.

But the truth was Houston was not the least sentimental about children. Or anything else. And yet even as he told himself that, he was aware of a feeling that he was a warrior going into battle on a completely unknown field, against a completely unknown enemy. Well, not completely. He knew what a powerful weapon her hair was on his beleaguered male senses. The touch of her skin. Now he could add dancing with her to the list of weapons in the arsenal she was so cheerfully using against him.

He rethought his plan to walk right into his fear. He might need a little time to regroup.

"Something has come up for tomorrow," he said. *It was called sanity.*

"You promised me two days," she reminded him. "I assume you are a man of honor."

More use of her arsenal. Challenging his *honor*.

"I didn't say consecutively."

She lifted an eyebrow, *knowing* the effect she was having on him, knowing she was chiseling away at his defenses.

"Friday?" he asked her.

"Friday it is."

"See you then," he said, as if he wasn't the least bit wary of what she had in store for him.

Tonight, and every other night this week, until Friday, he would hit the punching bag until the funny *yearning* that the glimpse of her world was causing in him was gone. He could force all the things he was feeling—*lonely, for one*—back into their proper compartments.

By the end of the week he would be himself again. He'd experienced a temporary letting down of his guard, but he recognized it now as a weakness. He'd had a whole lifetime of fighting the weaknesses in himself. There was no way one day with her could change that permanently.

Sparring with Molly Michaels was just like

boxing, without the bruises, of course. But as with boxing, even with day after day of practice, when it came to sparring, you could take a hair too long to resume the defensive position, and someone slipped a punch in. Rattled you. Knocked you off balance. It didn't mean you were going to lose that fight! It meant you were going to come back more aware of your defenses. More determined. Especially if the bell had rung between rounds and you had the luxury of a bit of a breather.

She wasn't going to wear him down, and he didn't care how many children she tried to use to do it.

CHAPTER SIX

HOUSTON WHITFORD congratulated himself on using his time between rounds wisely. By avoiding Molly Michaels.

And yet there really was no avoiding her. With each day at Second Chances, even as he busied himself researching, checking the new computer systems, okaying details of the renovations, there was no avoiding her influence in this place.

Molly Michaels was the sun that the moons circled around. Just as at the garden, she seemed to be the one people gravitated to with their confidences and concerns. She was warm, open and emotional.

The antithesis of what he was. But what was that they said? Opposites attract. And he could feel the pull of her even as he tried not to.

They had one very striking similarity. They

both wanted their own way, and were stubborn in the pursuit of it.

Tuesday morning three letters had been waiting for him on his desk when he arrived. The recurring theme of the three letters: *Why I Want a Prom Dress*. One was on pink paper. One smelled of perfume. And he was pretty sure one was stained with tears.

Wednesday there were half a dozen.

Yesterday, twenty or so.

Today he was so terrified of the basket overflowing with those heartfelt feminine outpourings that he had bypassed his office completely! The Sunshine and Lollipops program felt as if it had to be easier to handle than those letters!

Molly was chipping away at his hardheaded jadedness without even being in the same room with him.

Today children. He didn't really have a soft spot for children, but a few days ago he would have said the same of teenage girls pleading for prom dresses!

Molly was a force to be reckoned with. Houston was fairly certain if he was going to be here for two months instead of two weeks, by the end of that time he would be laying down his cloak over mud puddles for her. He'd probably be funding Prom Dreams out of his own pocket, just as he was donating the entire office renovation, and the time and skill of his Precision Solutions team.

The trick really was not to let Molly Michaels know that her charm was managing to permeate even his closed office door! The memory of the day they had already spent together seemed to be growing more vibrant with time instead of less.

Because she was a mischievous little minx— laughter seemed to follow in her wake—and she would not hesitate to use any perceived power over him to her full advantage!

So, the trick was not to let her know. They hailed a cab when she took one look at his car and pronounced it unsuitable for the neighborhood they were going into.

As someone who had once put a rock through a judge's very upscale Cadillac, Houston should have remembered that his car, a jet black Jaguar, would be a target for the angry, the greedy and the desperate in those very poor neighborhoods.

The daycare center was a cheery spot of color on a dreary street that reminded Houston of where he'd grown up. Except for the daycare, the buildings oozed neglect and desperation. The daycare, though, had its brick front painted a cheerful yellow, a mural of sunflowers snaked up to the second floor windows.

Inside was more cheer—walls and furniture painted in bright, primary colors. They met with the staff and Houston was given an enthusiastic overview of the programs Second Chances funded.

He was impressed by the careful shepherding of the funds, but how he'd seen people react to her in the garden was repeated here.

Dealing with people was clearly her territory. He could see this aspect of Second Chances was her absolute strength. There was an attitude of love and respect toward her that even a jaundiced old businessman like him could see the value of. Money could not buy the kind of devotion that Molly inspired.

Still, aside from that, analytically, it was clear to him Molly had made a tactical error in bringing him here. He had always felt this particular program, providing care for children of working or back-to-school moms, had indisputable merit. She had nothing to prove, here.

Obviously, in her effort to show him the soul of Second Chances she was trying to find her way to his heart.

And though she made some surprising headway, the terrible truth about Houston was that other women had tried to make him feel things he had no intention of feeling, had tried to unlock the secrets of his heart.

They had not been better women than Molly, but they had certainly been every bit as determined to make him feel something. He dated career women, female versions of himself, owned by their work, interested only in temporary diversion and companionship when it came to a relationship. Sometimes somebody wanted to change the rules partway in, thinking he should want what they had come to want: something deeper. A future. Together. Babies. Little white picket fences. Fairy tales. Forever.

Happily ever after.

He could think of very few things that were as terrifying to him. He must have made some kind of cynical sound because Molly glanced at him and smiled. There was something about that smile that made him realize she hadn't played all her cards yet.

"We're going to watch a musical presentation, and then have lunch with the children," she told him.

The children. Of course she was counting on them to bring light to his dark heart, to pave the way for older children, later, who needed prom dresses, though of course it was the *need* part that was open to question.

"Actually we could just—"

But the children were marching into the room, sending eager glances at their visitors, as excited as if they would be performing to visiting royalty.

He glared at Molly, just to let her know using the kids to try to get to him, to try to get her way, was the ultimate in cheesy. He met her gaze, and held it, to let her know that he was on to her. But before she fully got the seriousness of his stern look, several of the munchkins broke ranks and attacked her!

They flung themselves at her knees, wrapping sturdy arms around her with such force she stumbled down. The rest of the ranks broke, like water over a dam, flowing out toward the downed Molly and around her until he couldn't even see her anymore, lost in a wriggling mass of hugs and kisses and delightful squeals of *Miss Molly!*

Was she in danger? He watched in horror as Molly's arm came up and then disappeared again under a pile of wiggling little bodies, all trying to get a hold of her, deliver messy kisses and smudgy hugs.

He debated rescuing her, but a shout of laughter—female, adult—from somewhere in there let him know somehow she was okay under all that. Delighting in it, even.

He tried to remain indifferent, but he could not help but follow the faint trail of feeling within him, trying to identify what it was.

Envious, he arrived at with surprise. Oh, not of all those children, messy little beings that they were with their dripping noses and grubby hands, but somehow envious of her spontaneity, her ability to embrace the unexpected surprise of the moment, the gifts of hugs and kisses those children were plying her with.

Her giggles came out of the pile again. And he was envious of that, too. When was the last time he had laughed like that? Let go so completely to delight. Had he ever?

Would he ever? Probably not. He had felt a tug of that feeling in the garden, and again in Now and Zen. But when had he come to see feeling good as an enemy?

Maybe that's what happened when you shut down *feeling:* good and bad were both taken from you, the mind unable to distinguish.

Finally she extricated herself and stood up, though every one of her fingers and both her knees were claimed by small hands.

The businesswoman of this morning was erased. In her place was a woman with hair all over the place, her clothes smudged, one shoe missing, a nylon ruined.

And he had never, ever seen a woman so beautiful.

The jury was still out on whether she would make a good replacement for Miss Viv. So how could he know, he who avoided that particular entanglement the most—how could he know, so instantly, without a doubt, what a good mother Molly would make with her loving heart, and her laughter filled and spontaneous spirit?

And why did that thought squeeze his chest so hard for a moment he could not breathe?

Because of the cad who had made her suffer by letting her go, by stealing her dreams from her.

No, that was too altruistic. It wasn't about her. It was about him. He could feel something from the past looming over him, waiting to pounce.

As Molly rejoined him, Houston focused all his attention on the little messy ones trying so hard to form perfect ranks on a makeshift stage.

It was painfully obvious these would be among the city's neediest children. Some were in old clothes, meticulously cared for. Others were not so well cared for. Some looked rested and eager, others looked strangely tired, dejected.

With a shiver, he knew exactly which ones lay awake with wide eyes in the night, frightened of being left alone, or of the noises coming from outside or the next rooms. He looked longingly for the exit, but Molly, alarmingly intuitive, seemed to sense his desire to run for the door.

"They've been practicing for us!" she hissed at him, and he ordered himself to brace up, to face what he feared.

But why would he fear a small bunch of enthusiastic if ragamuffin children? He seated himself reluctantly in terribly uncomfortable tiny chairs, the cramped space ringing with children's shouts and shrieks, laughter. At the count of three the clamor of too enthusiastically played percussion instruments filled the room.

Houston winced from the racket, stole a glance at Molly and felt the horrible squeeze in his chest again. *What was that about?*

She was enchanted. Clapping, singing along, calling out encouragement. He looked at the children. Those children were playing just for her now. She was probably the mother each of them longed for: engaged, fully present to them, appreciative of their enthusiasm if not their musical talent.

And then he knew what it was about, the squeezing in his chest.

He remembered a little boy in ragged jeans, not the meticulously kept kind, at a school Christmas concert. He had been given such an important job. He was to put the baby Jesus in the manger at the very end of the performance. He kept pulling back the curtain. Knowing his dad would never come. But please, Mommy, please.

Hope turning to dust inside his heart as each moment passed, as each song finished and she did not enter the big crowded room. His big moment came and that little boy, the young Houston, took that doll that represented the baby Jesus and did not put him in the waiting crib. Instead, he threw it with all his might at all the parents who had come. The night was wrecked for him, he wanted to wreck it for everybody else.

Houston felt a cold shadow fall over him. He glanced at Molly, still entranced. He didn't care to know what a good mother she would be. It hurt him in some way. It made him feel as he had felt at the Christmas play that night. Like he wanted to destroy something.

Instead, he slipped his BlackBerry out of his pocket, scanned his e-mails. The Bradbury papers, nothing to do with Second Chances— all about his other life—had just been signed. It was a deal that would mean a million and a half dollars to his company. Yesterday that would have thrilled him. Filled him.

Yesterday, before he had heard her laughter emerge from under a pile of children, and instantly and without his permission started redefining everything that was important about his life.

He shook off that feeling of having glimpsed something really important—maybe the only thing that was important—he shook it off the same way he shook off a punch that rattled him nearly right off his feet. Deliberately he turned his attention to the small piece of electronics that fit in the palm of his hand.

Houston Whitford opened the next e-mail. The Chardon account was looking good, too.

Molly congratulated herself on the timing of their arrival at the daycare program. The concert had been a delight of crashing cymbals, clicking sticks, wildly jangling triangles. Now it was snack time for the members of the rhythm section, three and four year olds.

They were so irresistible! They were fighting for her hands, and she gave in, allowed herself to be tugged toward the kitchen.

She glanced back at Houston. He was trailing behind. How could he be looking at his BlackBerry? Was she failing to enchant him, failing to make him *see?*

Well, there was still time with her small army of charmers, and Molly had never seen a more delightful snack. She felt a swell of pride that Second Chances provided the funding so that these little ones could get something healthy into them at least once a day.

Healthy but fun. The snack was so messy that the two long tables were covered in plastic, and the children, about ten at each long, low table, soon had bibs fashioned out of plastic grocery bags over their clothes.

On each table were large plastic bowls containing thinly cut vegetables—red and green peppers, celery, carrots—interspersed with dips bowls mounded with salad dressing.

The children were soon creating their own snacks—plunging the veggies first into the dressing, and then rolling the coated veggie on flat trays that held layers of sunflower seeds, poppy seeds, raisins.

Though most of the children were spotlessly clean beneath those bibs and the girls all had hairdos that spoke of tender loving care, their clothes were often worn, some pairs of jeans patched many times. The shoes told the real story—worn through, frayed, broken laces tied in knots, vibrant colors long since faded.

Molly couldn't help but glance at Houston's

shoes. Chuck had been a shoe aficionado. He'd shown her a pair on the Internet once that he thought might make a lovely gift from her. A Testoni Norvegese—at about fifteen hundred dollars a pop!

Was that what Houston was wearing? If not, it was certainly something in the same league. What hope did she have of convincing him of the immeasurable good in these small projects when his world was obviously so far removed from this he couldn't even comprehend it?

She had to get him out of the BlackBerry! She wished she had a little dirt to throw on those shoes, to coax the happiness out of him. She had to make him *see* what was important. This little daycare was just a microcosm of everything Second Chances did. If he could feel the love, even for a second, everything would change. Molly knew it.

"Houston, I saved you a seat," she called, patting the tiny chair beside her.

He glanced over, looked aghast, looked longingly—and not for the first time—at the exit door. And then a look came over his face—not of a man joining preschoolers for snack—but of a warrior striding toward battle, a gladiator into the ring.

The children became quite quiet, watching him.

If he knew his suit was in danger, he never let on. Without any hesitation at all, he pulled up the teeny chair beside Molly, hung his jacket over the back of it—not even out of range of the fingers, despite the subtle Giorgio Armani label revealed in the back of it—and plunked himself down.

The children eyed him with wide-eyed surprise, silent and shy.

Children, Molly told herself, were not charmed by the same things as adults. They did not care about his watch or his shoes, the label in the back of that jacket.

Show me who you really are.

She passed him a red pepper, a silly thing to expect to show you a person. He looked at it, looked at her, seemed to be deciding something. She was only aware of how tense he had been when she saw his shoulders shift slightly, saw the corners of his mouth relax.

Ignoring the children who were gawking at him, Houston picked up a slice of red pepper and studied it. "What should I do with this?"

"Put stuff on it!"

He followed the instructions he could understand, until the original red pepper was not visible any longer but coated and double coated with toppings.

Finally he could delay the moment of truth no longer. But he did not bite into his own crazy creation.

Instead, he held it out, an inch from Molly's lips. "My lady," he said smoothly. "You first."

Something shivered in her. How could this be? Surrounded by squealing children, suddenly everything faded. It was a moment she'd imagined in her weaker times. Was there anything more romantic than eating from another's hand?

Somehow that simple act of sharing food was the epitome of trust and connection.

She had wanted to bring him out of himself, and instead he was turning the tables on her!

Molly leaned forward and bit into the raisin-encrusted red pepper. She had to close her eyes against the pleasure of what she tasted.

"Ambrosia," she declared, and opened her eyes to see him looking at her with understandable quizzicalness.

"My turn!" She loaded a piece of celery with every ingredient on the table.

"I hate celery," he said when she held it up to him.

"You're setting an example!" she warned him.

He cast his eyes around the table, looked momentarily rebellious, then nipped the piece of celery out of her fingers with his teeth.

Way too easy to imagine this same scenario in very different circumstances. Maybe he could, too, because his silver-shaded eyes took on a smoky look that was unmistakably sensual.

How could this be happening? Time standing still, something in her heart going crazy, in the middle of the situation least like any romantic scenario she had ever imagined, and Molly was guilty of imagining many of them!

But then that moment was gone as the children raced each other creating concoctions for their honored guests. As when his shoulders had relaxed, now Molly noticed another layer of some finally held tension leaving him as he surrendered to the children, and to the moment.

They were calling orders to him, the commands quick and thick. "Dunk it." "Roll it." "Put stuff on it! Like this!"

One of the bolder older boys got up and pressed right in beside Houston. He anchored himself—one sticky little hand right on the suit jacket hanging on the back of the chair—and leaned forward. He held out the offering—a carrot dripping with dressing and seeds—to Houston. Some of it appeared to plop onto those beautiful shoes.

Molly could see a greasy print across the shoulder lining of the jacket.

A man who owned a suit like that was not going to be impressed with its destruction, not able to see *soul* through all this!

But Houston didn't seem to care that his

clothes were getting wrecked. He wasn't backing away. After his initial horror in the children, he seemed to be easing up a little. He didn't even make an attempt to move the jacket out of harm's way.

In fact he looked faintly pleased as he took the carrot that had been offered and chomped on it thoughtfully.

"Excellent," he proclaimed.

After that any remaining shyness from the children dissolved. Houston selected another carrot, globbed dressing on it and hesitated over his finishing choices.

The children yelled out suggestions, and he listened and obeyed each one until that carrot was so coated in stuff that it was no longer recognizable. He popped the whole concoction in his mouth. He closed his eyes, chewed very slowly and then sighed.

"Delicious," he exclaimed.

Molly stared at him, aware of the shift happening in her. It was different than when they had chased each other in the garden, it was different than when they had danced and she was entranced.

Beyond the sternness of his demeanor, she saw someone capable of exquisite tenderness, an amazing ability to be sensitive. Even sweet.

Molly was sure if he knew that—that she could see tender sweetness in him—he would withdraw instantly. So she looked away, but then, was compelled to look back. She felt like someone who had been drinking brackish water their entire life, and who had suddenly tasted something clear and pure instead.

The little girl beside Houston, wide-eyed and silent, held up her celery stick to him—half-chewed, sloppy with dressing and seeds—plainly an offering. He took it with grave politeness, popped it in his moth, repeated the exaggerated sigh of enjoyment.

"Thank you, princess."

Her eyes grew wider. "Me princess," she said, mulling it over gravely. And then she smiled, her smile radiant and adoring.

Children, of course, saw through veneers so much easier than adults did!

I am allowing myself to be charmed, Molly warned herself sternly. And of course, it was even more potent because Houston was not trying to charm anyone, slipping into this role as naturally and unselfconsciously as if he'd been born to play it.

But damn it, who wouldn't be charmed, seeing that self-assured man give himself over to those children?

I could love him. Molly was stunned as the renegade thought blasted through her brain.

Stop it, she ordered herself. She was here to achieve a goal.

She wanted him to acknowledge there was the potential for joy anywhere, in any circumstance at all. Bringing that shining moment to people who had had too few of them was the soul of Second Chances. It was what they did so well.

But all of that, all her motives, were fading so quickly as she continued to *see* something about Houston Whitford that made her feel weak with longing.

He couldn't keep up with children hand-making him tidbits. In minutes he had every child in the room demanding his attention. He solemnly accepted the offerings, treated each as if it was a culinary adventure from the five-star restaurant he was dressed for.

He began to really let loose—something Molly sensed was very rare in this extremely controlled man. He began to narrate his culinary adventure, causing spasms of laughter from the children, and from her.

He did Bugs Bunny impressions. He asked for recipes. He used words she would have to look up in the dictionary.

And then he laughed.

Just like he had laughed in the garden. It was possibly the richest sound she had ever heard, deep, genuine, true.

She thought of all the times she had convinced Chuck to do "fun" things with her, the thing she deemed an in-love couple should do that week. Roller-skating, bike riding, days on the beaches of Long Island, a skiing holiday in Vermont. Usually paid for by her of course, and falling desperately short of her expectations.

Always, she had so carefully set up the picture,

trying to make herself feel some kind of magic that had been promised to her in songs, and in movies and in storybooks.

Molly had tried so hard to manufacture the exact feeling she was experiencing in this moment. She had thought if she managed this outing correctly she would show Houston Whitford the real Second Chances.

What she had not expected was to see Houston Whitford so clearly, to see how a human being could shine.

What if this was what was most real about him? What if this was him, this man who was so unexpectedly full of laughter and light around these children?

What if he was one of those rare men who were made to be daddies? Funny, playful, able to fully engage with children?

"I told you, you don't laugh enough," she whispered to him.

"Ah, Miss Molly, it's hard for me to admit you might be right." And then he smiled at her, and it seemed as if the whole world faded and it was just the two of them in this room, sharing something deep and splendid.

Molly found herself wanting to capture these moments, to hold them, to keep them. She remembered the camera he had given her, took it out and clicked as he took a very mashed celery stick from a child.

"The best yet," she heard him say. "To die for. But I can't eat another bite. Not one."

But he took one more anyway, and then he closed his eyes, and patted his flat belly, pretending to push it out against his hand. The children howled with laughter. She took another picture, and Molly laughed, too, at his antics, but underneath her laughter was a growing awareness.

She had thought bringing Houston to her projects would show her the real Houston Whitford. And that was true.

Unfortunately, if this laughing carefree man was the real Houston, it made her new boss even more attractive, not less! It made her way too aware of the Molly that had never been put behind her after all—the Molly who yearned and longed, and ultimately *believed.*

"Will you stay for story time?"

No. Nothing that ended happily-ever-after! Please! She suddenly wanted to get him out of here. Felt as if something about her plot to win his heart was backfiring badly. She had wanted to win him over for Second Chances! Not for herself.

He was winning her heart instead of her winning his, and it had not a single thing to do with Second Chances.

"Not possible," Molly said, quickly, urgently. "Sorry."

It wasn't on the schedule to stay, thank goodness, but even before the children started begging him, it seemed every one of them tugging on some part of him to get him up off the floor, his eyes met Molly's and she knew they weren't going anywhere.

With handprints and food stains all over the pristine white of that shirt, Houston allowed himself to be dragged to the sinks, where he obediently washed his own hands, and then one by one helped each of the children wash theirs.

After he washed "Princess's" face, the same child who had sat beside him at snack, she crooked her finger at him. He bent down, obviously thinking, as Molly did, that the tiny tot had some important secret to tell him.

Instead she kissed him noisily on his cheek.

Molly held out the camera, framed the exquisite moment. *Click*.

He straightened slowly, blushing wildly.

Click. She found herself hoping that she was an accomplished enough photographer to capture that look on his face.

"Did you turn me into a prince, little princess?" Houston asked.

The girl regarded him solemnly. "No."

But that's not how Molly felt, at all. A man she had been determined to see as a toad had turned into a prince before her eyes.

Again she realized that this excursion was not telling her as much about Houston Whitford as it was telling her about herself.

She wanted the things she had always wanted, more desperately than ever.

And that sense of desperation only grew as Molly watched as Houston, captive now, like Gulliver in the land of little people, was led over to the story area. He chose to sit on the floor, all the children crowding around him. By the time they were settled each of those children seemed to have claimed some small part of him, to touch, even if it was just the exquisitely crafted soft leather of his shoe. His "little princess" crawled into his lap, plopped her thumb in her mouth and promptly went to sleep.

Molly could not have said what one of those stories was about by the time they left a half hour later, Houston handing over the still sleeping child.

As she watched him, she was in the grip of a tenderness so acute it felt as if her throat was closing.

Molly was stunned. The thing she had been trying to avoid because she knew how badly it would weaken her—was exactly what she had been brought.

She was seeing Houston Whitford in the context of family. Watching him, she *felt* his strength, his protectiveness, his *heart*.

She had waited her whole life to feel this exquisite tenderness for another person.

It was all wrong. There was no candlelight. It smelled suspiciously like the little girl might have had an accident in her sleep.

Love was supposed to come first. And then these moments of glory.

What did it mean? That she had experienced such a moment for Houston? Did it mean love would come next? That she could fall in love with this complicated man who was her boss?

No, that was exactly what she was not doing! No more wishing, dreaming! Being held prisoner by fantasies.

No more.

But as she looked at him handing over that sleeping little girl, it felt like she was being blinded by the light in him, drawn to the power and warmth of it.

Moth to flame, Molly chastised herself ineffectively.

"Sorry she's so clingy," the daycare staff member who relieved him of her said. "She's going through a rough time, poor mite. Her mother hasn't been around for a few days. Her granny is picking her up."

And just like that, the light she had seen in his face snapped off, replaced by something as cold as the other light had been warm.

Selfishly, Molly wanted to see only the warmth, especially once it was gone. She wanted to draw it back out of him. Would it seem just as real outside as it had in? Maybe she had just imagined it. She had to know.

She had to test herself against this fierce new challenge.

As they waited for a cab on the sidewalk, he seemed coolly remote. The electronic device was back out. She remembered this from yesterday. He came forward, and then he retreated.

"You were a hit with those kids." She tried to get him back to the man she had seen at lunch.

He snorted with self-derision, didn't look up. "Starving for male attention."

"I can see you as a wonderful daddy some-day," she said.

He looked up then, gave her his full attention, a look that was withering.

"The last thing I would ever want to be is a daddy," he said.

"But why?"

"Because there is quite a bit more to it than carrot sticks and storybooks."

"Yes?"

"Like being there. Day in and day out. Putting another person first forever. Do I look like the kind of guy who puts other people first?"

"You did in there."

"Well, I'm not."

"You seem angry."

"No kidding."

"Houston, what's wrong?"

"There's a little girl in there whose mom has abandoned her. How does something like that happen? How could anybody not love her? Not want her? How could anybody who had a beautiful child like that not devote their entire life to protecting her and making her safe and happy?"

"An excellent daddy," she said softly.

"No, I wouldn't," he said, coldly angry. "Can you wait for the cab yourself? I just thought of something I need to do."

And he left, walking down the street, fearless, as though that fancy watch and those shoes didn't make him a target.

Look at the way he walked. He was no target. No victim.

She debated calling after him that she had other things on the agenda for today. But she didn't. This was his pattern. She recognized it clearly now.

He felt something. Then he tried to walk away, tried to reerect his barriers, his formidable defenses, against it.

Why? What had happened to him that made a world alone seem so preferable to one shared?

"Wait," she called. "I'll walk with you."

And he turned and watched her come toward

him, waited, almost as if he was relieved that he was not going to carry some of the burden he carried alone.

CHAPTER SEVEN

HOUSTON watched Molly walking fast to catch up with him. The truth was all he wanted was an hour or so on his punching bag. Though maybe he waited, instead of continuing to walk, because the punching bag had not done him nearly the good he had hoped it would last night. Now it felt as if it was the only place to defuse his fury.

That beautiful little girl's mother didn't want her. He knew he was kidding himself that his anger was at *her* mother.

From the moment he'd heard Molly laughing from under the pile of children a powerless longing for something he was never going to have had pulled at him.

You thought you left something behind you, but you never quite left that. The longing for the love of a mother.

The love of his mother. She was dead now. He'd hired a private detective a few years back to find her. Somehow he had known she was dead. Because he'd always thought she would come back. He would have left Beebee's world in a minute if his mother had loved him and needed him.

It had been a temporary relief when the private eye had told him. Drugs. An overdose.

Death. The only reasonable explanation for a mother who had never looked back. Except, as the P.I. filled in the dates and details, it wasn't the explanation he'd been seeking after all. She'd died only a few years before he made the inquiries about her—plenty of time to check in on her son if she had wanted to.

She hadn't.

And he was powerless over that, too.

There was nothing a man of action like Houston hated so much as that word. *Powerless.*

Molly came and walked beside him. He deliberately walked fast enough to keep her a little breathless; he knew intuitively she would have a woman's desire to *talk,* to probe his wounds.

He could feel his anger dispersing as they left the edgier part of the Lower East Side and headed back to where Second Chances was in the East Village.

"This is where I live," she said as they came to a well-kept five-story brownstone. "Do you want to stop for a minute? Meet Baldy? Have a coffee?"

She obviously intended to pursue this thing. His *feelings*. He was not going to meet her bird, enter her personal space and have a coffee with her!

On the other hand, the punching bag had not been working its normal magic. He hesitated. And she read that as a yes. In the blink of an eye she was at the door with her key out.

He still had a chance to back away, but for some reason he didn't. In fact, he ordered himself to keep walking, to call after her, *Maybe some other time*. But he didn't.

Instead, feeling oddly *powerless* again, as if she might have something he was looking for, he followed her up the three flights of stairs to her apartment.

"Close it quick," she said, as he came through the door behind her. "Baldy."

And sure enough out of the darkness of the apartment a tiny missile flew at them, a piece of flesh-colored putty with naked wings. It landed on her shoulder, pecked at her ear, turned and gave him a baleful look.

"Good grief," he said, but he was already glad he had come. The bird was so ugly he was cute. The tiny being's obvious adoration for Molly lightened something in Houston's mood. "ET call home!"

Still, there was something about that bird, looking as if it, too, would protect her to the death, that tugged at a heart that had just faced one too many challenges today.

The bird rode on her shoulder as she guided him into the apartment which looked to be all of five hundred square feet of pure feminine coziness.

The bird kissed her cheek and made a whimpering noise that was near human. She absently stroked his featherless body with a tender finger. The bird preened.

"Just have a seat," she said. "I'll make coffee."

But he didn't have a seat. Instead he questioned his sanity for coming in here. He studied the framed poster of a balloon rising over the Napa Valley in California. He turned away from it. How was it her humble five hundred square feet felt like *home* in a way he had never quite managed to achieve?

It must be the fresh flowers on the coffee table between the two sofas.

"Nice flowers," he heard himself say.

"Oh, I treat myself," she called from the kitchen. "There's a vendor on the way home from work."

He went and stood in the doorway of her tiny kitchen, watched her work.

"No boyfriend buying you flowers?"

That's exactly why it had been a mistake to accept her invitation into her personal space. This was going too far. He'd chased her with a worm. And danced with her. He'd felt the exquisite plumpness of her lip on his finger when he'd fed her from his hand. Now he was in her house.

In high school, he scoffed at himself, that might count as a relationship. But for a mature man?

"Believe me," she muttered, "the boyfriend I had never bought me flowers."

"Really?" he said, and some of his dismay at that must have come through in his tone. What kind of cad wouldn't buy her flowers? He would buy her flowers if he was her boyfriend.

Now that was a dangerous side road his mind had just gone down!

Her tongue was caught between her teeth as she concentrated on putting coffee things on a tray. She pressed by him in the narrow doorway, set the tray on the coffee table by the flowers.

It all looked very cozy. He went and sat down.

She poured coffee. "He was more than my boyfriend. My fiancé."

"Ah." He took a generous gulp of coffee, burned his mouth, set it down and glared at it.

She took a tiny sip of hers. "His name was Chuck. We were supposed to get married and live happily ever after. Instead, he emptied my bank account and went to live on a beach in Costa Rica. That's what finished me for being a romantic."

Why was she telling him this? He got it very suddenly. They were going to share confidences.

"Now I see it as a good thing," she said. "It got me ready for you."

He stared.

"Hardened me," she declared. "So that I'm not a romantic anymore. So that I can handle all the changes at work."

And he wasn't aware he had stopped breathing until he started again. For a suspended moment in time, he had thought she was going to say losing her fiancé had freed her to love him. What would give him such a notion?

Still, it was very hard not to laugh at her declaration that she was *hardened*. "But there's such a thing as being too hard," she went on.

"I guess there is," he agreed warily.

"I'd like you to trust me. Tell me why the situation at the daycare with the little girl and her mother made you so angry today?"

Her perception—the feeling that she could see what he least wanted to be seen—was frightening.

What was even more frightening was the temptation that clawed at his throat. To take off all the armor, and lay it at her feet. Tell her all of it. But the words stuck.

"When I was little," she told him, still thinking it was a confidences exchange, "my mom and dad fought all the time. And I dreamed of belonging to a family where everyone loved each other."

"Ah," he said, unforthcoming.

"Do you think such a family exists?"

"Honestly? No."

"You're very cynical about families, Houston. Why?"

She wanted to know? Okay, he'd tell her. She probably wasn't going to be nearly as happy to know about him as she thought she was going to be!

"Because I grew up in one just like yours. Constant fighting. Drama. Chaos. Actually it would probably make yours look like something off a Christmas card. And it made me feel the opposite of you. Not a longing for love. An allergy to it."

"Isn't that lonely?"

He didn't answer for a long time. "Maybe," he finally said. "But not as lonely as waiting for something that never happens. That's the loneliest."

"What did you wait for that never happened?"

This was what he had come here for. For her to coax this out of him.

He was silent.

"Trust me," she said quietly.

And he could not resist her. Even though he pitted his whole strength against it, he heard himself say, his voice a low growl of remembered pain, "Once, when I was quite small, I was in a Christmas concert."

And somehow he told her all of it. And with every single word it felt like a chain that had been wrapped hard around his heart was breaking apart, link by link.

Somehow, when he was finished, she had moved from the couch across from him to the place right beside him. Her hand was in his. And she was silent for the longest time.

"But why didn't she come?" she finally asked.

"I don't know," he said. "I don't remember."

"Was it just that once that she didn't come?" Here she was dragging more out of him.

"No, it was all the time."

"Because she couldn't care about anybody but herself," Molly said sadly. "Did you think it was about you?"

As she spoke those words Houston knew a truth he did not want to know. Of course he had thought it was about him.

It was not his father he had never forgiven. Not entirely.

Somewhere in him, he had always thought the truth was that he was a person no one could care about. Not if tested. Not over time. If his own mother had found him unworthy of love, that was probably the truth.

It was not his mother he had not forgiven, either.

It was himself he had never forgiven. For not

being worthy of love. For not being a person that his mother and father could have at least tried to hold it all together for.

Molly reached up and guided his hand to her face. It was wet with her tears. It was such a tender powerful gesture, without words.

Something in him surrendered. He allowed himself to feel something he had not felt for a very long time. At home. As if he belonged. As if finally, in this world, there was one place, one person who could accept him for what he was.

He contemplated the temptation to tell her more, not sure if a man could put things back the way they used to be after he had experienced such a thing as this.

And it felt like a weakness that he could not fight and that he was not sure if he wanted to.

Damn it, he wanted to. He could not give in to this.

But then, his hand that rested on the wetness of her cheek went, it seemed of its own volition, to the puffiness of her lip. He traced the fullness of it with his thumb, took in the wideness of her eyes, the gentle puff of her breath touching his thumb.

I'm going to kiss her, he thought, entranced. Dismayed.

He snapped back from her, dropped his hand from the full and exquisite temptation of her lips.

But she wasn't having it. When he pulled away, she stretched forward. She had clearly seen what he would have loved to have kept hidden. In every sense.

Her lips grazed his. Tender. Soft. Supple.

Sexy.

It took every ounce of his considerable discipline to pull away from her. He got to his feet, abruptly, aware if he stayed on that couch with her he was not going to be fully in control of what happened next.

"That shouldn't have happened," he said gruffly.

"Why?" she said softly.

She knew why. She knew she was crashing through his barriers faster than he could rebuild them.

"It was inappropriate. I apologize."

"I think it was me who kissed you. And I'm not apologizing."

"Molly, you have no idea what you are playing with," he told her softly, sternly.

"Maybe I do."

As if she saw him more clearly than he saw himself! Just because he had told her one thing. He didn't like it that he had told her that. That brief moment of feeling unburdened, not so damned lonely, was swiftly changing to regret.

"I have work to do," he said, hardened himself to what these moments had made him feel, turned and walked away, shutting the door firmly behind him.

But he didn't go back to Second Chances, despite his claim he had work to do. He also had no work at home, not even his laptop. He didn't even feel compelled to check his BlackBerry. Life could go on without him for one evening.

He was sitting out on his terrace, overlooking Central Park.

The terrace was as beautifully furnished as

his apartment, dark rattan furniture with deep white cushions, plants flowering in a glorious abundance of color under the new warmth of the spring sun.

Houston was sipping a glass of wine, a Romanée-Conti from the Burgundy region of France. The wine was so rare and sought after it had to be purchased in boxes that contained a dozen bottles of wine, only one the coveted Romanée-Conti, the other eleven from other domains.

For as spectacular as the wine was, it occurred to him this was the kind of wine that seemed as if it would lend itself to romance.

Over the sounds of the traffic, he could hear the pleasant *clip clop* of the hooves of a horse pulling a carriage.

For the second time—unusual since Houston was not a man given to romantic thoughts—his mind turned to romance. He wondered if young lovers, or honeymooners, in New York for the first time—were riding in that carriage.

He wondered if they were full of hope and optimism, were enjoying the spring evening, snuggled under a blanket, the world looking brighter because they were seeing it through that lens of love. He resisted an impulse to go give them the remainder of that exquisite bottle of wine.

Houston realized, not happily, that he felt lonely. That the merest touch of Molly's lips had unleashed something terrifying in him.

He realized, too, that he usually kept his life crammed full enough that he could avoid feelings like that—a sudden longing to share a moment like this one with someone else.

Molly Michaels if he wanted to get specific. The truth was they had shared some moments that had forged an instant sense of bonding, of intimacy. It was hard to leave it behind. That was all. It was natural to feel this way.

But it wasn't natural for *him* to feel this way.

He realized he still had Molly's camera in his pocket, and he took it out, scanned idly through the pictures.

He stopped at the one where *Princess* was kissing his cheek.

Something had changed for him, Houston acknowledged, in that exact moment. Because at that moment, he had surprised himself. He had surprised himself by so clearly seeing—no, not just seeing, *knowing*—the need in those children. But the biggest surprise had come when he had embraced that need instead of walking—no, running—away from it.

Everything had become personal after that.

It hadn't been about helping out Beebee and Miss Viv anymore, doing his civic duty, get in, get out, goodbye.

Those kids in that daycare, wistful for the fathers and mothers they didn't have, had hurt him, reminded him of things long buried, which made the fact he'd embraced their need even more surprising to him.

They called to who he had once been, and he wondered if there was something in that self he had left behind that had value.

"I doubt it," he muttered, wanting a beer out of a bottle being a prime example. The fact that, even though he was doing nothing else tonight, he was avoiding answering the letter from his father, being another example.

Houston wished, suddenly, wearily, that he had delegated the whole Second Chances project to someone else. It was bringing things to the surface that he had been content to leave behind for a long time.

He scanned through more pictures on the camera, stopped at the one of Molly that he had taken in the garden. She was leaning on the shovel, a smudge of dirt on her cheek, her hair wild around her, her eyes laughing, the constant wariness finally, finally gone from them.

Some tension she always held around him had relaxed in that garden. The playful part that he had glimpsed the first time he had seen her—in a bridal gown at work—had come back out at the garden. And at the preschool.

People loved her. That was evident in the next picture, her in the very middle of a line of ancient grandmothers, unaware how her youth and vitality set her apart, how beautiful she looked with her head thrown back in laughter as she kicked her leg up impossibly high. And in another of her at Sunshine and Lollipops, of her laughing, unaware there was salad dressing in her hair.

Ah, well, that was the promise that had been in her eyes all along. That she could take a life that had become too damned serious and insert some fun back in it.

What would she add to an evening like this one? Would she be content to sit here, listening to spring sounds? Or would she want to be out there, part of it?

Houston thought of the taste of her lips beneath his—raindrop fresh—and felt a shiver of pure longing that he killed.

Because the bigger question was what *price* would he pay to know those things? Would it be too high?

"Ah, Houston," he said. "The question isn't whether the price you would pay would be too high. It's what price would be asked of her, and if it would be more than she was willing to pay?"

Because to satisfy his curiosity by inviting her into his life would only invite trouble. Eventually she would want things he could not give her.

Because you could not give what you did not know. What you had never known. Though he felt how disappointed Beebee would be to know that even her best efforts had not taught him the lesson she most wanted to give him. That a life well lived was rarely lived alone.

And certainly not without love.

She had really come along too late. He'd been fourteen, his life lessons already learned, his personality long since shaped.

He tossed back a wine that was meant to be savored. He did not want to even think the word *love* on the same day he had told her things he had never told another living soul.

Told her? Ha! Had it dragged out of him!

He got up abruptly, went inside, closed the French doors on the sounds of spring unfolding relentlessly all around him.

He thought of her guiding his hand to the tears slipping down her cheeks, and something happened that hadn't happened to him since he had learned his mother was dead.

A fist closed in his throat, and something stung behind his eyes.

That's what he needed to remember about love, he told himself sternly. It hurt. It hurt like hell. It could make a strong man like his father weak.

Or a strong man like him.

A man needed to approach these kinds of temptations with a plan, with a road map of how to extricate himself from sticky situations.

And so when he saw her next, he would be coolly professional. He would take a step back from all the lines that had been crossed. He would not think of chasing her with a worm, or dancing with her, or holding her and telling her one small secret. He would not think of how it had felt to open his world just a little bit to another human being.

He steeled himself against the temptation to go those few steps down the hall to her office, just to see her, make small talk, ask about the stupid budgie.

So, when she arrived in the doorway of his office just before lunch the next day, he hardened himself to how beautiful she looked in a white linen suit, a sunshine-yellow top, her hair already doing its escape routine.

He had one more week here, and then he was never going to see her again. He could suck it up for that long.

"They finished painting my office yesterday," she said, cheerfully, as if her lips had not touched his. "The ochre isn't that bad."

"That's good." Apparently she had decided she could suck it up for that long, too. Keep it professional, talk about paint, not revisit last night. *Is that why it had taken her so long to come and see him today?*

"I was at the Suits for Success auction this morning."

As if he had asked why he hadn't seen her!

"How was it?"

"Great."

They stood on a precipice. Were they going to go deeper? Were they going to remember last night or move on?

She jumped off it.

"My bird likes you," she said, and then she smiled. "He doesn't like everybody."

Her bird liked him? Wasn't she thinking about that kiss? Had it been a sympathy kiss, then? Good grief!

"That's good." How ridiculous was it to preen slightly because her bird liked him? And didn't like just anybody? Houston fought the urge to ask her if the bird had liked Chuck, as if he could use that to judge the bird's true skill.

"I want you to know it meant a lot to me. The whole day yesterday. Letting me show you the soul of Second Chances." Her voice dropped lower. "And then showing me a bit of yours."

"I don't like pity, Molly."

"Pity?" She looked genuinely astounded, and then she laughed. "Oh, my God, Houston, I cannot think of a man who would inspire pity less than you."

And he could tell that she meant it. And that the kiss had not been about pity at all. And she was so beautiful when she laughed.

Houston knew he could not spend another day with her. She made him too vulnerable. She opened something in him that was better left

closed. He could not be with her without looking at her lips and remembering.

The research portion of the job at Second
Chances was done. He knew exactly what each
store brought in, he knew what their staffing
and overhead costs were, he'd assigned a management team to go in and help them stream-
line, improve their efficiency, develop marketing
plans.

One week left. He could suck it up for that
long if he avoided her. If he stayed in Miss
Viv's newly revamped office with the door
firmly shut and the Do Not Disturb sign out.

Houston Whitford had built a career on his
ability to be in control.

But this week was showing him something
different about himself. And that version of himself could not refuse what she was offering.

One week. There were really two ways of
looking at it. He could avoid her. Or he could
engage with her.

Why not give himself that?

Because it's dumb, his more reasonable self
said, *like playing with fire.*

But he felt the exquisite freedom of a man who had just ripped up his plan and thrown away the map. Like he could do anything and go anywhere.

For one week.

"Do you want to go for lunch?"

Molly was beaming at him. The late morning light was playing off her hair, making the copper shimmer with flame and reminding him what it was like to play with fire, why children were drawn to sticks in campfires. Because before fire burned, it was irresistible, the temptation of what it offered wiping out any thought of consequences.

Molly didn't taste one single bite of the five-star meal she had ordered. She didn't think of Miss Viv, or Prom Dreams or what the future of Second Chances was going to look like with him as the boss.

When she left him after lunch, she felt as if she was on pins and needles waiting to see him again, *dying* to see him again. Thinking uncontrollable thoughts of how his lips had felt beneath hers.

Was he feeling it, too?

When her phone rang, and it was him, she could hear something in his voice.

"I noticed that boys' soccer team we sponsor are playing on the Great Lawn fields at Central Park tonight. That's close to home for me. I wouldn't mind going."

With me?

"With you."

There was a momentary temptation to manufacture an exciting full schedule to impress him, to play hard to get, but she had played all the games before and knew they were empty. What she wanted now was real.

"I'd love to join you," she said.

And that's how they ended up spending most of the week together. The soccer game—where she screamed until she was hoarse—led to dinner. Then he said he had been given tickets for *Phantom of the Opera* for the next evening. Though it was the longest running show in Broadway history, Molly hadn't seen it, and was thrilled to go with him.

After, she was delighted when he insisted on seeing her home. And then said, "If I promise to be a perfect gentleman, can I come in and see Baldy?"

He came in. She made coffee. Baldy decided to give him a chance. She was not sure she had ever seen anyone laugh so hard as when Baldy began to peck affectionately on Houston's ear.

Being with Houston was easy and exhilarating. She found herself sharing things with him that she had rarely told anyone. She told him about the pets that had preexisted Baldy. She told him things from her childhood, anecdotes about the long chain of step-fathers. Finally it was he who remembered they both had to work in the morning.

He hesitated at her door. For a moment she thought he would kiss her, again, and her life as she had known it would be over because she knew they were reaching the point where neither of them was going to be able to hold back.

But clearly, though the struggle was apparent

in his face, he remembered his promise to be a gentleman.

At work the next day, she appreciated his discipline. It was hard enough to separate the personal from the professional without the complication of another kiss between them.

But even without that complication her life suddenly felt as if it were lit from within.

They had gone from being combatants to being a team. They were working together, sharing a vision for Second Chances. Houston could make her laugh harder than she had ever laughed. He could take an ordinary moment and make it seem as if it had been infused with sunshine.

There was so much to be done and so little time left to do it as they moved toward the re-opening of the office, the open house unveiling party set for Friday afternoon. The personal and the professional began to blend seamlessly. They worked side by side, late into the night, eating dinner together. He always walked her home when they were done.

She was beginning to see how right he had

been about Second Chances, it could be so much better than she had ever dreamed possible.

And her personal life felt the same way. Life could be so much better than she had ever dreamed was possible!

It seemed like a long, long time ago, she had tried on that wedding dress, and felt all that it stood for. In this week of breathtaking changes and astounding togetherness, Molly had felt each of those things. *Souls joined. Laughter shared. Long conversations. Lonely no more.*

Was she falling in love with her boss? She had known the potential was there and now she evaluated how she was feeling.

If falling in love meant feeling gloriously alive every minute you spent together, then yes. If falling in love meant noticing a person's eyes were the exact color of silver of moonlight on water, yes. If falling in love was living for an accidental brush of a hand, yes.

If falling in love made the most ordinary things—coffee in the morning, the phone ringing and his voice being on the other end—extraordinary, then yes.

She glanced up to see him standing in her office doorway, looking at her. Something in his face made a shiver go up and down her spine.

"Tomorrow's the big day," she said, smiling at him.

But he didn't smile back.

"Molly, I need to show you something."

There was something grim about him that stopped the smile on her lips. He ushered her outside to a waiting cab, and gave the driver an address she didn't recognize.

But somehow her gut told her they were going somewhere she did not want to go.

CHAPTER EIGHT

HOUSTON knew something that Molly didn't. Their time together was ticking down. Only Houston was so aware now that the week he had given himself didn't seem like enough. He was greedy. He wanted more. A woman like her made a man feel as if he could never get enough of her. Never.

Giving himself that week had made him feel like a man who had been told he only had a week to live: on fire with life, intensely engaged, as awake as he had ever been.

But there was that shadow, too. A feeling of foreboding from knowing that thing that she didn't. Nothing good ever lasted.

He realized the thought of not seeing her was like putting away the sun, turning his world, for all its accomplishments, for all he had acquired, back into a gray and dreary space, not unlike this neighborhood they were now entering.

He was not sure when he had decided to take this chance, only that he had, and now he was committed to it, even though his spirits sank as they got closer to the place that he had called home, and that somehow, he had never left behind. This was the biggest chance of his life.

What if he let her know the truth of him? All of it?

"I want to show you something," he said to her again as the cab slowed and then stopped in front of the address he had given the driver. He helped her out of it. She was, he knew, used to tough neighborhoods. But there were certain places even the saints of Second Chances feared to go.

"This is Clinton," he said, watching her face. "They don't call it Hell's Kitchen anymore."

The cab drove away, eager to be out of this part of town.

"You've found us a new project?" she asked. She had the good sense to frown at the cab leaving.

Maybe a project so challenging even Molly would not want to take it on.

"Not exactly. This is where I grew up."

"This building?"

He scanned her face for signs of reaction. He was aware pity felt as though it would kill him. But there was no sign of pity in her face, just the dawning of something else, as if she knew better than him why he would bring her here.

Why had he? A test.

"Yes. I want to show you something else." He walked her down the street. "This didn't used to be a liquor store," he told her quietly. "It used to be a bank."

She waited, and he could tell she knew something was coming, something big. And that she wanted it to come. Maybe had waited for this. He plunged on, even while part of him wanted to back away from this.

"When I was fourteen my dad lost his job. Again. My mother was her normal sympathetic self, screaming at him he was a loser, threatening to trade up to someone with more promise."

Again, he scanned her face. If *that* look came across it, the drowned kitten look, like he needed rescuing by *her,* they were out of here.

"He took a gun, and he came down here and he held that gun to the teller's nose and he took all the money that poor frightened woman could stuff into a bag. On his way out, a man tried to stop him. My father shot him. Thankfully he didn't kill him.

"He went to jail. Within a week my mother had traded up as promised. I never saw her again."

"But what happened to you?" Molly whispered.

"I became the kind of bitter man who doesn't trust anyone or anything."

"Houston, that's not true," she said firmly. "That's not even close to true."

He remembered the first day he had met her, when he had talked about being hungry and out of work and not having a place to live, had talked about it generically but her eyes had still been on his face, *knowing*.

"What is true then?" he asked her roughly. What if she *really* knew? He was aware of holding his breath, as if he had waited his whole life to find out.

Her eyes were the clearest shade of green he had ever seen as she gazed at him. A small smile touched her lips, and she took a step toward him, placed her hand on his chest, her palm flat, the strength of her *knowing* radiating from her touch.

"This is true," she whispered. "Your heart."

And the strangest thing was that he believed her. That somewhere in him, safe from the chaos, his heart had beat true and strong.

Whole.

Waiting.

"Did you think this would change how I feel about you?" she asked softly.

It was a major distraction. How *did* she feel about him?

"I always knew there was something about you that made you stronger than most people," she said.

He suddenly knew why he was here. He was asking her, *are you willing to take a chance on me?* And it was only fair that she knew the whole story before she made that decision. Still, he made one last ditch effort to convince her she might be making a mistake.

"There's nothing romantic about growing up like this, Molly. Maybe it makes you strong. Or maybe just hard. I have scars that might never heal."

"Like the one on your nose?"

"That's the one that shows."

"I think love can heal anything," she said quietly, and somehow it felt as if she had just told him how she felt about him, after all.

Something felt tight in his chest. She was the one who believed in miracles. And standing here at the heart of Clinton, seeing the look in her eyes, it occurred to him that maybe he did, too.

"There's something else you should know," he said stubbornly. *Tell her all of it.*

"What's that?" she said, and she was looking at him as if not a single thing he could ever do or say could frighten her away from him.

Houston hesitated, searching for the words, framing them in his mind.

My father's getting out of prison. I don't know what to do. Somehow I feel that you'll know what to do, if I let you into my world. Did she want to come into this?

He drank her in, felt her hand still on his heart. The softness in her face, the utter desire to love him, could make a man take a sledgehammer to his own defenses, knock them down, not be worried about what got out. Wanting to let something else in. Wanting to let in what he saw in her eyes when she looked at him.

A place where a man could rest, and be lonely no more. A place where a man could feel cared about. A place where he could lay down his weapons and fight no more. A place where he could be seen. And *known*. For who he was. All of it. She would want him to answer that letter from his father. He knew a man who was going to be worthy of loving her would be able to do that.

Would be able to believe that love could heal all things, just as she had said.

For a moment he was completely lost in thought, the look in her eyes that believed him to be a better man than Houston Whitford had ever believed himself to be. A man could rise up to meet that expectation, a man could live in the place that he found himself. Funny, that he would come this close to heaven in Clinton.

Suddenly the hair on the back of his neck went up. He was aware of something trying to penetrate the light that was beginning to pierce his darkness. And then he realized he was not free from darkness. This world held a darkness of its own, not so easy to escape, and he foolishly had brought her here.

They weren't alone on this street. The hair rising on the back of his neck, an instinctual residue from his days here, let him know they were being watched.

He glanced over Molly's shoulder, moved away from her hand still covering his heart. With the focused stare of a predator, a man in a blue ball cap nearly lost in the shadow of the liquor store's doorway was watching them. He glanced away as soon as Houston spotted him.

What had Houston been thinking bringing her here? Flashing his watch and his custom suit like a neon invitation. He knew better than that! He should have known better than that.

That man pushed himself off the wall, shuffled by them, eyed Houston's watch, scanned his face.

Houston absorbed the details. The man was huge, at least an inch taller than Houston, and no doubt outweighed him by a good fifty pounds. He had rings on his hand, a T-shirt that said Jay on it, in huge letters. His face was wily, lined with hardness.

"What's going on?" Molly asked, seeing the change in Houston's face. She glanced at the man, back at him.

But Houston didn't answer, preparing himself, his instincts on red alert.

"Got the time?" "Jay" had circled back on them.

The certainty of what would happen next filled Houston. Mentally he picked up the weapons he had thought it was safe to lay down. Without taking his eyes off Jay he noted the sounds around him, the motion. The neighborhood was unusually quiet today, and besides, people here knew how to mind their own business.

Molly was looking up at the thug, smiling, intent on seeing the good in him, just as she was intent on seeing the good in everyone. *Even a man who had come into her life to bring changes she hadn't wanted.*

Except falling in love. She'd wanted that. The bridal gown should have warned him. He should have backed away while he still could have. Because Molly was about to see something of him that he had not intended to show her. That he thought he had managed to kill within himself.

She looked at her wrist, gave "Jay" the time. Houston was silent, reading the predatory readiness in that man's body language, the threat.

Silently he begged for Molly to pay attention to her intuition, to never mind hurting anyone's feelings if she was wrong. He wanted her to run, to get the hell out of the way. To not see what was going to happen next.

"How bout a cigarette?" the man asked.

The first doubt crossed Molly's features.

Houston could feel her looking at him for direction, but he dared not take his eyes off "Jay," not for a second.

"I don't smoke," she said uneasily.

Adrenaline rushed through Houston. In one smooth move he had taken Molly and shoved her behind his back, inserted himself between her and the threat.

"He doesn't want a cigarette, Molly," he said, still not taking his eyes from the man.

"Ain't no watch worth you dying for," the man told him, and Houston saw the flash of a silver blade appear in his palm.

"Or you," Houston said.

Molly gasped. "Just give him the watch."

But if "Jay" got the watch, then what? Then the purse? Then the wallet? Then Molly?

The watch might not be worth dying for. But other things were.

"Just give it up," the man was saying in a reasonable tone of voice. "No one has to get hurt."

Something primal swept Houston. He went to a place without thought, a place of pure instinct.

Years on the speed bag had made him lightning fast.

He knew his own speed and he knew his own strength, and there was nothing in him that held back from using them both. He was outgunned, the man both taller and heavier than him. There could be no holding back. None.

He was aware his breath was harsh, but that he felt calm, something at his core beyond calm. Still. It felt strangely as if this was the moment he'd prepared for his entire life, all those hours at the bag, running on cold mornings, practicing the grueling left right combinations and jabs.

All for this. To be ready for this one moment when he had to protect Molly.

"Hey, man," the guy said, "give it up, I tell you."

But the phrase was only intended to distract. Peripherally Houston registered the silvery flash in the young thug's hand, the glitter of malice in his eyes. Houston was, in a split second, a man he had never wanted Molly to see, a man he had never wanted to see himself, even as he'd been aware of the shadowy presence within him.

This was what he had tried to outrun, the violence of his father, the primitive ability to kill thrumming through his veins. He was a man who had never left these streets behind him at all, who was ready now to claim the toughness, the resilience, the resourcefulness that a person never really left behind them.

His fists flashed. Left jab. Straight right. The man slashed at him once, but his heaviness made him less than agile, and Houston's fury knew no bounds. Jay went down under the hail of fists, crashed to the sidewalk.

Houston was on top of him, some instinct howling within him. *Don't let him get up. Not until you see the knife. Where is it?*

Pounding, pounding in the rhythm to the waves of red energy that pulsed through him. The fury drove his fists into the crumpled form of Jay over and over.

Slowly he became aware that Molly was pulling at him, trying to get him off him, screaming.

"Stop, Houston. You're going to kill him."

"Where's the knife?"

And then he saw it, the silver blade under Jay's leg. The man had probably dropped it the minute he'd been hit.

Still, Houston was aware of his reluctance, as he came back to her, made himself stop, rose to his feet, tried to shake it off.

He was aware he had come here to show Molly where he was from, to see how she reacted to that.

Instead, he had found out who he really was. A thug. Someone who could lose control in the blink of an eye. He'd brought Molly down here to see if she could handle *his* reality. He was grateful this test that not even he could have predicted or expected had come.

They were not going to move forward. There was no relationship with Molly Michaels in his future.

What if he got this angry at her? The way his father had gotten angry at his mother? And claimed it was love.

And if anybody asked him why he had just pulverized that young man, wouldn't that be his answer, too?

Because he loved her.

And he would protect her with his very life.

Even if that meant protecting her from himself.

He had come so close to believing he could have it all. Now watching that dream fade, he felt bereft.

The man rolled to his side, scrambled drunkenly to his feet, sent a bewildered look back, blood splashing down a nose that was surely broken onto a shirt. The knife lay abandoned on the sidewalk.

Only when he was sure that Jay was gone did Houston turn to her. She stared at him silently. And then her face crumpled. A sob escaped her and then another. She began to shake like a leaf. She crept into him, laid her head against his chest and cried.

Just the shock of the assault? Or because she had seen something in him that she couldn't handle and that love could not tame, had no hope of healing?

Houston took off his jacket and wrapped it around her shoulders, pulled her close into him, aware of how fragile she was, how very, very feminine, how his breath stirred her hair.

There was that exquisite moment of heightened awareness where it felt as if he was breathing her essence into his lungs.

To savor. To hold inside him forever. Once he said goodbye.

And then, out of nowhere, heaven sent, a cab pulled up and he shoved her in it.

"B-b-but shouldn't we wait for the police?"

The police? No, when you grew up in these neighborhoods you never quite got clear of the feeling that the police were not your friends.

Besides, what if some nosy reporter was monitoring the scanner? What a great story that would make. CEO of successful company wins fight with street thug. But just a bit of digging could make the story even more interesting. A nineteen-year-old story of a bank robbery.

Loser, his mother had screamed when there was another lost job, another Friday with no paycheck. The look on her face of such disdain. And the look on his father's.

I will win her. I will show her. I will show them all.

Except he hadn't. His father had been his mother's hero for all of two hours, already drunk, throwing money around carelessly. The police had arrived and taken him. An innocent bystander shot, but not, thank God, killed, during the bank robbery his father had committed. *Nineteen years of a life spent for an attempt to win what Houston realized, only just now, could not be won.*

"No police," he said firmly. "Give the driver your address."

It was a mark of just how shaken she was that she didn't even argue with him, but gave her address and then collapsed against him, her tears warming his skin right though his shirt. His hand found her hair. Was there a moment in the last few days when he had not thought of how her hair felt?

Touching it now felt like a homecoming he could not hold on to. Because in the end, wasn't love the most out of control thing of all?

And yet he could not deny, as he held her,

that that's what the fierce protectiveness that thrummed through him felt like. As if he would die protecting her if he had to, without hesitation, without fear.

A feeling was coming over him, a surge of endorphins releasing like a drug into his brain and body.

He would have whatever she gave him tonight. He would savor it, store it in a safe place in his heart that he could return to again and again.

Once it was over. And it would be over soon enough. He did not have to rush that moment.

He helped her up the stairs to her apartment. Her hands were shaking so badly he had to take the keys from her.

"Do you have something to drink?" he asked, looking at her pale face.

"Zinfandel," she said. "Some kind of chicken zinfandel."

"And I always thought wine was made with grapes."

He hoped to make her laugh, but somehow his tone didn't quite make it. Tonight he had gone down there with an expectation of *maybe* there being some kind of chance for them.

For him to build a life different than the one of unabating loneliness he had always known. A life different than what his family had given him.

But that fury resided in him. And he was not sharing that legacy with her. Someday, if he followed that look in her eyes, there would be children, too. They did not deserve the Whitford legacy, either. Innocent. His unborn children were innocent, as once he had been innocent.

The ugly truth now? He had *liked* the feeling of his fist smashing into that man's face.

He would have liked to just leave, but he could tell she was quickly disintegrating toward shock.

"I think we need something a little stronger than chicken zinfandel," he suggested.

"I think there might be some brandy above the fridge. Chuck drank..." she giggled "...everything."

She was staring at him with something hungry in her eyes. She reached out and touched him, her hand sliding along the still coiled muscle of his forearm. There was naked appreciation in her touch.

He recognized in her a kind of survivor euphoria. He felt it sometimes after a sparring match. A release of chemical endorphins, a hit of happiness that opened your senses wide.

Tomorrow she would wake up and think of his hands smashing into that man, and feel the fear and doubt that deserved.

Tonight, she would think he was her hero.

He pulled his arm away from her, poured her a generous shot of brandy, made her drink it, but he refused one for himself.

One loss of control for the night was quite enough.

"Houston." She took a sip, stared at him, drank him as greedily as the brandy. And he let her. Drank her back, saved her every feature, the wideness of her eyes and the softness of her lips.

"I think you're bleeding," she gasped suddenly.

He followed her gaze down. A thin thread of red was appearing above the belly line on his white shirt. So, the knife had not dropped instantly. At some level, had the physical threat triggered his rage?

Excuses.

"You're hurt," she said, frightened.

If he was, adrenaline was keeping him from feeling it. "Nah. A little scrape. Nothing. A long way from the heart."

If his arm was hanging by a thread at the moment he suspected he would do the manly thing and tell her it was nothing.

"Let me see."

"No, I'm okay."

But she pointed at a chair, and because he was going to savor every single thing she gave him tonight—he sat there obediently while she retrieved the first aid kit. "Take off your shirt," she told him.

Who had he been kidding when he'd said his injuries were not close to the heart? It was all about the heart. The walls he had tried to repair around it were crumbling again, faster than he could build them back up.

Now his heart was going to rule his head. Because he knew better than to take off that shirt for her. He was leaving. Why drag this out?

And he did it anyway, aware he was trying to memorize the kindness of her face, and the softness in her eyes, the hunger in her.

He undid the buttons with unreasonable slowness, dragging out this moment, torturing himself with the fact it would not be him who fed that hunger. He let the shirt fall open. He didn't need to take it off, but he did, sliding it over his shoulders, holding it loosely in one hand. The tangy scent of his own sweat filled the room, and he watched her nostrils flare, drinking him in.

She knelt in front of him, and her scent, lemony and clean, melted into his. Even though she was trying to be all business, he could see the finely held tension in her as her eyes moved over his naked chest.

It seemed like a long time ago that he had first seen her, known somehow she would change something about him.

Make him long for things he could not have.

But he could have never foreseen how this moment of her caring for him would undo him.

Her tenderness toward him created an ache, a powerful yearning that no man, not even a warrior, could fight.

Not forever.

And he had been fighting since his hand had first tangled in her hair, had found the zipper on her wedding dress.

"Oooh," she said, inspecting the damage, a tiny thin line that ran vertically from just below his breastbone to his belly button. "That's nasty."

He glanced down. To him it looked like a kitten scratch.

"Are you sure we shouldn't call the police?" she said. "You've been stabbed."

"No police."

"I don't understand that."

"You wouldn't understand it," he said harshly. "All it would take would be for one snoopy reporter to be monitoring the police channel, and it could be front page news. What a nice human interest story. Especially if anyone did any digging. The son of an armed robber foils an armed robbery."

"Your father's shame isn't yours."

"Yes, it is," he said wearily. "You know after my dad was arrested, and my mom left, I got a second chance. A great foster home. For the first time in my life I had food and clothes and security.

"Then in high school there was a dance. I danced with a cheerleader. Cutest girl in the school. And some guy—maybe her boyfriend, or just a hopeful, I don't remember—came and asked her what she was doing dancing with a thug.

"And I nearly killed him. Just the way I nearly killed that man tonight. And I liked the way it felt. Just the way my dad must have liked the way it felt when he was hitting people, which was often."

"I don't believe that," she said uncertainly. "That you liked it. You just did what you had to do. He was huge. Any kind of holding back might have turned the tide in his favor."

He laughed, aware of the harsh edge to it. "That was the first two punches. He was already done when he hit the ground."

"Houston, you did an honorable thing tonight.

Why are you trying to change it into something else?"

"No," he said softly. "Why are you?"

"I'm not."

"Yes, you are. Because you always want to believe the best about everybody even if it's not true."

"How come you haven't spent your life beating people up if you like it so darn much?"

"I learned to channel my aggression. Boxing."

"There you go."

"Not because I wanted to," he said, "but because I didn't like the way people looked at me after that had happened."

"You want to be a bad guy, Houston. But you're just not."

He got up even though she wasn't finished. He could not allow her to convince him. He knew what he was. He knew what he had felt when he hit that man. Satisfaction. Pure primal satisfaction. He tugged his shirt on. "I have to go."

"Please don't."

That man could see through her veneers as

ruthlessly as he had disposed of his own. That man saw everything that she wanted to hide.

Her need was naked in her eyes, in the shallowness of her breath, in the delicate color that blossomed in her cheeks, in the nervous hand that tried to tame a piece of that wild hair.

Her gaze locked on to his own, her green eyes magnificent with wonder and hunger and invitation.

He was aware of reaching deep inside himself to tame the part of him that just wanted to have her, own her, possess her, the two sides of his soul doing battle over her.

He took a step toward the door. She stepped in front of him. Took his shoulders, stood on her tiptoes.

Her lips grazed his lips. He had waited for this moment since he had tasted her the first time. He felt the astonishing delicacy of her kiss, and the instant taming of that thing in him that was fierce.

Not all the strength of his warrior heart could make him back away. He had promised himself he would take whatever she offered tonight, so he would have something to savor in the world he was going back to.

So he took her lips with astounding gentleness and a brand-new part of him, a part he had no idea existed, came forward. It met her tenderness with his own. Exploring what she offered to him with reverence, recognition of the sacredness of the ritual he had just entered into.

This was the dance of all time. It was an ancient call that guaranteed the future. It was a place where ruthless need and tender discovery met, melded and became something brand-new.

His possession of her deepened. With a groan, he allowed his hands to tangle in her hair, to draw her in nearer to him. He dropped his head from the warm rhapsody of her mouth, and trailed kisses down the slender column of her throat, to the hollow at the base of it.

With his lips, he could feel her life beating beneath that tender skin.

"Please," she whispered, her hands in his hair, on his neck.

Please what? Stop, or go forward?

His lips released her neck, and when that

contact stopped, it was as if the enchantment broke. Some rational part of him—the analytical part that had been his presenting characteristic, his greatest strength, his key to his every success—studied her.

The half-closed eyes, the puffiness of the lips, the pulse beating crazily in her throat.

Storing it.

But an unwelcome truth penetrated what he was feeling. He could not take what she had to offer, for just one night. You didn't just kiss a woman like her and walk away from it unscathed, as if it was nothing, meant nothing, changed nothing.

She would be damaged by such a cavalier *taking* of her gifts.

Besides, she was not fully aware of what she was offering. The brandy on top of the shock had made her vulnerable, incapable of making a rational decision. If there was ever a time the rational part of him needed to step up to the plate it was now.

He was not the hero she wanted to see.

"I'm going," he said.

"Please don't," she said. "I'm scared. I know it's silly, but I feel scared. I don't want to be alone."

Perhaps he could be a hero for just a little while longer, though it would take all that was left of his strength.

It was so hard to press her head into his chest, let his hands wander that magnificent hair. It was hard to move to the couch, to allow her to relax into him, to feel her shallow breathing become deep and steady, to let her feel safe.

He had another fault then, as well as fury that years had not tamed. He was no hero, but a thief, because he was going to steal this moment from her.

Steal it to hold in his heart forever.

After a long time, her grip relaxed on his hand, her lips opened and little puffed sighs escaped. She had gone to sleep on him. He slipped out from underneath her sweet weight, laid her on the couch, looked for something to cover her with.

He tucked a knitted afghan around her, looked at her face, touched her hair one more time.

He glanced around her apartment, noticed the

poster on the wall, and was mesmerized by it for a moment. He took a deep breath and moved away from all it represented.

Though he was now beyond weariness, he went back to his office, the one he would turn over to Miss Viv tomorrow.

There was a new stack of letters in defense of Prom Dreams. Just in case he wasn't feeling bad enough, he read them all.

A picture fell out of the last one. It was of a beautiful young woman, at her university convocation. The podium she was standing by said Harvard.

Dear Mr. Whitford:

I recently heard that Second Chances was thinking about canceling their Prom Dreams program. I would just like you to know that five years ago, my school was chosen to participate in that program. You may find this hard to believe, but being allowed to choose that beautiful dress for myself was the first time in my life that I ever felt I was worth something.

He set the letter down.

No, he came from the very neighborhood her school had been in. He knew how hard it was to feel as if you were worth something.

He knew, suddenly, that was as important as having a full belly. Maybe more. Because filling a belly was temporary. Making a person feel as if they were worth something, even for a moment, that was something they carried in them forever.

He could not have Molly. He had decided that tonight.

But still, he could live up to the man she had hoped he was. It could be a standard that he tried to rise to daily. Even as it was ending, something in him could begin.

It could start with leaving a note to Miss Viv, telling her that Molly should lead this organization into its new future, that she had gifts greater than his to give Second Chances. The ability to analyze was nothing compared to the ability to love that she poured into this place.

It could start with a few prom dresses.

And it could start with an answered letter to his father.

CHAPTER NINE

IT WAS way too soon to love him, Molly thought, walking up the street toward the office the next morning.

But there was no doubt in her mind that she was in love. Totally. Irrevocably. Wonderfully.

The whole world this morning felt different, as if rain had come and washed it clean, made it sparkle.

He had brought her to the place of his birth, thinking he risked something by showing her everything. Instead, she had seen him so completely it made her heart stand still, awed to be in the presence of a soul so magnificent, so strong.

She smiled thinking of how he thought it said something *bad* about him that he had dispensed with that horrible young mugger so thoroughly.

She suspected she would spend the rest of her life performing alchemy on him, showing him what he thought was lead was really gold.

Molly shivered when she thought of him last night *protecting* her. Prepared to die to protect her if he had to. And then running that act of such honor and such incredible bravery through the warp of something in his own mind, and making it *bad*.

He said he had lost control. But she didn't see it that way. He'd stopped. If he'd truly lost control, "Jay" would never have gotten up and scrambled away.

Houston didn't lose control.

If he did, last night would have ended much differently! Molly was aware of feeling a little singing inside of her as she contemplated the delightful job she was going to have making that man lose control.

She was pretty sure it was going to involve lots of lips on lips, and that she was up for the job. Even thinking about it, her belly did the most delightful downward swoop, anticipating seeing him today.

Maybe she'd dispense with the niceties, just close his office door and throw herself at him.

Wantonly. There was going to have to be an element of taking him by surprise to make him lose control.

Then again, today was a big day for them, a milestone, the unveiling of the new Second Chances that they had created together, that they would continue to create together.

Maybe she would hold off taking him by surprise until the open house was over. But she'd tease him until then. The odd little touch, her eyes on him, a whisper when he least expected it.

Her life felt so full of exciting potential. She could barely believe her life had gone from that dull feeling of same-same to this sense of invigorated engagement in such a short time.

That's what love did.

Brought out the best. Empowered. Made all things possible. And healed all things, too.

Molly could feel her heart beating a painfully quick tattoo within her chest as she mounted the stairs, and went in the front door of the office.

Another day together. A gift. If things had gone differently last night they might not have this gift. It was a reminder to live to the fullest, to take the kind of chances that made a life shimmer with glory.

Tish was already at her desk. She looked up, beaming.

"There's a surprise for you."

Molly's eyes went to the huge bouquet of pink lilies on Tish's desk. She started to smile.

When she'd woken last night and found he had slipped away, she had thought maybe he planned to try to fight this thing. She put her nose to the flowers, and let subtle scent engulf her.

But no, they were on the same page. He was going to romance her. It was probably going to be hard for a realist like him, too! Because lovely as they were, flowers weren't going to cut it. They were the easiest form of romance.

Tish laughed. "Those aren't for you, silly. Those are from the next door neighbor congratulating us on our reopening. Your surprise is in Miss Viv's office."

He was waiting for her, then. Had some

surprise to make up for the disappointment of a kiss not completed, of not staying the night with her.

She went to the closed office door, knocked lightly, opened it without waiting for an answer.

A sight that should have filled her heart to overflowing greeted her. Miss Viv sat behind her own desk.

Molly bit back the wail, *Where is he?* and rushed into the arms that were open to her. She had to fight back tears as Miss Viv's embrace closed around her.

"My word," Miss Viv said. "Isn't this incredible? Isn't the office incredible? You'll have to show me how to use this."

"I thought you didn't like computers?" Molly teased.

"There isn't anything here I don't like," Miss Viv declared happily.

"Where's Houston?" Molly asked, casually.

"I'm not sure," Miss Viv said. "I haven't seen him. Do you press this button to put the camera on? Molly, help me figure this out!"

Molly complied, pulled a chair up to Miss Viv's desk. Part of her was fully engaged in showing Miss Viv how to use the computer, hearing tidbits about her trip and the wonderful time she'd had.

Part of her listened, waited. Part of her asked, *Where is his office going to be, now that Miss Viv is back?*

She waited for the sound of the voice and the footsteps that did not come. For some reason, she thought of the time he had told her about waiting at the concert for his mother. This, then, was how he had felt.

The waiting was playing with her game plan. She was not going to be able to contain herself when she finally saw him. She was surely going to explode with joy. Everyone was going to know.

And she didn't care.

But by lunch he still had not come. Molly tried his cell phone number. She got the recording.

She listened to his voice, *greedily,* hung up because she could not think of a message to leave that could begin to say how she was feeling.

Eventually she and Miss Viv joined the rest of the office in getting ready for the open house. The flowers on Tish's desk had only been the first of many arrangements that arrived: from friends of Second Chances, neighboring businesses, well-known New York business people and personalities.

The caterers arrived and began setting up food, wine and cheese trays, while Brianna went into a tizzy of last minute arranging and "staging," as she called it.

At three, people began to trickle in the door. Invited guests, curious people from the neighborhood, the press. Information packets had been prepared for all of them: what Second Chances did, complete with photographs. Though no mention of a donation was ever made, each packet contained a discreet cream envelope addressed to Second Chances.

Molly felt as though she was in a dream as that first trickle of people turned into a flood. She was there, and not there. She was answering questions. She was engaged with people. She was laughing. She was enjoying the sense of triumph of a job well done. She was sipping the champagne that had been uncorked, nibbling on the incredible variety of cheeses and fresh fruits.

But she was aware she was not there at all.

Watching the door. Waiting.

Where was he? Where was Houston? This was his doing, the success of this gathering— and there was no doubt it was a success—was a tribute to his talent, his hard work, his dedication, his leadership. How could he not be here to reap the rewards of this, to see that basket on Tish's desk filling up with those creamy white envelopes?

Finally Miss Viv asked for everyone's attention. She thanked them all for coming, and invited them to watch a special presentation with her.

The lights were lowered, the voices quieted.

A screen came down from the ceiling.

Music began to play.

The office designer who had been in Molly's

office closet the first day stood beside Molly. "Wait until you see this," she said. "Mr. Whitford always does the most incredible presentations." Then she cocked her head. "Hey, he's changed the music. That's interesting. It was Pachelbel before."

But it wasn't Pachelbel now. It was a guitar, and a single voice, soulful, almost sorrowful, filling the room, as black and white pictures began to fill the screen, one melting into the next one.

"You told me," the music said, "that I would know heaven."

But the pictures weren't of heaven. They were of dark streets and broken windows, playgrounds made of asphalt, boarded over businesses. They were of the places, that Molly had found out yesterday, where he had grown up.

The places that had shaped that amazingly strong, wonderful man.

The voice sang on, "You promised me a land free from want…"

And the pictures showed those who had newly

arrived, the faces of immigrants, wise eyes, un-smiling faces, ragged clothes.

"I expected something different than what
I got,
Oh, Lord, where is my heaven, where is my
heaven?"

The pictures were breathtaking in their com-position: a young man crying over the body of a friend in his arms, a little boy kicking a can, shoulders humped over, dejection in every line of him, a woman sitting on steps with a baby, her eyes fierce and afraid as she looked into the camera.

Then the pictures began to change, in perfect sync with the tempo of the music changing, the lyrics suspended, a single guitar picking away at the melody, but faster now, the sadness leaving it.

The pictures showed each of the stores, Peggy laughing over a rack of clothes at Now and Zen, the ultrasophisticated storefront of Wow and Then, a crowded day at Now and Again. Then it showed this office before the makeover, walls coming down, transformation.

And that voice singing, full of hope and power now, singing, *If we just come together, if I see you as my brother, Lord, there is my heaven, there is my heaven.*

Now there was a photograph of the green space that Molly recognized as her garden project, the only color in a block of black and white, the children at the daycare, the Bookworms bus.

Emotion was sweeping the room. Brianna was dabbing at her eyes with a hankie. "Oh, my God," she whispered, "he's outdone himself this time."

Something in Molly registered that. *This time.* Brushed it away like a pesky fly that was spoiling an otherwise perfect moment. Except it wasn't perfect. Because he wasn't here.

"Where is Houston?" Molly whispered to Brianna. She *needed* him to be here, she needed to be sharing this with him.

"Oh," Brianna said, "he never comes to the final day."

"Excuse me? What final day? He's the boss

here." *We are going to be building a future together.*

And hopefully not just at work.

But Brianna was clapping now, keeping time. Every one was clapping, keeping time as that voice sang out, rich and powerful, full of promise, *"There is my heaven."*

A final picture went across the screen.

It was that little girl, the princess, kissing Houston on the cheek.

And Molly thought, as that picture froze in its frame, *there is my heaven.*

Over the thunder of applause, she turned to ask Brianna what she meant, about the final day. About Houston never coming to the final day.

Other thoughts were crowding her memory. She realized he had a relationship with all those workers who had come in, with Brianna. He hadn't just met them when he took over, hadn't just hired contractors and designers and computer geeks.

He'd known them all before.

He *never* came to the final day. He's outdone himself *this time.*

Houston Whitford had done all this before. That's why he'd been brought in to Second Chances. Because he'd done it all before. And done it well.

The applause finally died down. Miss Viv stood at the front of the room, beaming, dabbing at her eyes.

As she spoke, Molly felt herself growing colder and colder.

"First of all, I must thank Houston Whitford for donating his time, his expertise and his company, Precision Solutions, to all of us here. I know his team does not come cheaply. His donation probably rates in the tens of thousands of dollars."

The cold feeling increased. He'd been donating all the renovations? He'd let her believe he was taking the money from Prom Dreams?

No, he'd never said that. He'd probably never told Molly an out-and-out lie. The more subtle kinds of lies. The lies of omission.

"Houston's not here today," Miss Viv said. "With any luck he's back to his real job. Personally I wish Precision Solutions was consulting with the president of the United States about getting this country back on track."

A ripple of appreciative laughter, only Molly wasn't laughing. There. It was confirmed. He was not an employee, not the new head of Second Chances. He had never planned to stay, he had known all along they were not building a future of any kind together.

The only one, apparently, who had not known that was her.

Little Molly Pushover. Whose record of being betrayed by every single person she had ever loved was holding.

Miss Viv was talking about the holidays she had just gone on, and how it had made her rethink her priorities. She had decided to retire. Then Miss Viv was thanking everyone for their years of support, hoping they would all show the same support and love to the new boss as they had shown to her.

"I'd like to introduce you now to our new leader," Miss Viv said, "the person I trust to do this job more than anyone in the world."

So, he was here after all. Molly allowed relief

to sweep over her. She must have misunderstood. He was leaving Precision Solutions to head up Second Chances. Molly could feel herself holding her breath, waiting to see him, *dying* to see him.

So relieved because as the afternoon had worn on and he had not shown up, a feeling of despair had settled over her. She had known *exactly* what he had felt like at that Christmas concert when his mother had not come.

He would not make someone else feel like that. Not that he cared about. He wouldn't. She thought of the look of fierce protectiveness on his face last night. He would never be the one to hurt her. He had almost died to keep her safe!

But now he was here. Somewhere. She craned her neck, waiting for Miss Viv to call his name. After the crowds had thinned, she would laugh with him about her misunderstanding. Kick closed that office door, and see what happened next.

But Miss Viv didn't call his name.

Her eyes searched the people gathered around

her, until she finally found Molly. She smiled and held out her hand.

"Molly, come up here."

Molly tried to shrink away. Oh, no, she did not want to be part of introducing the new boss. She thought her feelings would be too naked in her face, she felt as if there was no place for her to hide.

But Miss Viv did not notice Molly trying to shrink away. She gestured her forward even more enthusiastically. She thought Molly not coming was because of the press of the crowds, and gave up trying to get her to the front.

The crowd opened for her. Somebody pushed her from behind.

Molly had no choice but to go up there.

"I'd like to introduce you to the new head of Second Chances," Miss Viv said gleefully. "Molly Michaels."

Molly stood there, stunned. There was no happiness at all. Just a growing sense of self-scorn. Until the very last minute, she had believed in him, believed the best in him. Just like always.

No doubt she'd be getting another postcard from some far off exotic place soon. To rub her face in her own lack of discernment.

Her own Pollyanna need to *believe*.

She had been lied to by the man she thought she had seen more truly than anyone else. He wasn't the boss and he wasn't going to be part of her future here.

Or anywhere else.

"I don't know that I'm qualified," Molly managed to say through stiff lips, in an undertone to Miss Viv.

"Oh, but you are, dear. That's one of the things our darling Houston was here to do. To find out if you were ready to take over for me."

Our darling Houston.

Molly had been falling in love, and he'd been conducting a two week job interview?

The front door opened, and a delivery man walked in, barely able to see over his arms loaded with long, white boxes. "Where should I put—" He stopped, uncomfortably aware he was the center of attention. "The dresses?"

"What dresses?" Tish asked.

"I hate to break up the party, but I got a truck-load of prom dresses out there, lady, and I'm double parked."

Miss Viv put a hand to her heart. "Oh," she said, and her eyes filled with fresh tears. "My Houston."

And again, Molly felt no joy at all. *Her Houston. Darling Houston.* Houston Whitford was Miss Viv's Houston.

They had a relationship that preexisted his coming here. He had never thought to mention that in two weeks, either. Nor had Miss Viv mentioned it when she had first introduced him.

Molly had been lied to, not just by him, but by the woman she loved more than any other in the world?

Somehow Molly managed to get through the gradual wind-down of the festivities. She begged off looking at the dresses that had arrived. Someone else could do it. Prom Dreams seemed like a project suited to a desperate romantic, which she wasn't going to be anymore.

And she meant that, this time. That moment

in the garden when Molly had thought she knew who she really was wavered like the mirage that it was.

Though there were still people there, Molly tried to get out the door unnoticed.

Miss Viv broke away from the crowd and came to her. "Wait just a sec. Houston left something for you."

She came back moments later with a long, narrow box, pressed it into Molly's unwilling hands.

"Are you all right?"

She was not ready to discuss the magnitude of how not all right she was. "Just tired," she said.

"Are you going to open it?"

Molly shook her head. "At home." The fact that it was light as a feather should have warned her what was in it.

She opened the box in the safety of her apartment with trepidation rather than enjoyment.

There was the feather boa she had worn on that day when they had danced at Now and Zen. Baldy's feathers. One of those fancy dresses, a diamond ring, flowers, somehow she could have handled a gift like that. Expensive. Impersonal somehow. A *thanks for the memories* brush off.

But this?

Molly allowed the tears to come. What she should have remembered when she was nourishing the ridiculous fantasy of him as the lone gunslinger who saved the town, was how that story always ended.

With the hero who had saved the town riding away as alone as the day he had first ridden in.

An hour ago watching Houston's face flash across the screen, that child kissing his cheek, Molly had thought, *there is my heaven.*

How was it that heaven could be so close to hell?

CHAPTER TEN

HOUSTON awoke with the dream of her kiss on his lips. If he closed his eyes again, he could conjure it.

It had been a month since he had felt her lips under his own, since he had known he had to say goodbye to her. Why were the memories of the short time they had shared becoming more vivid instead of fading?

Probably because of the choice he had made. He might have chosen to walk away from Molly—for her own good—but he had also chosen not to walk away from her lesson.

Every day he tried to do one thing that would make her proud of him, if she knew, one thing that somehow made him live up to the belief he had seen shining in her eyes.

He had sent a truckload of brand-new shoes to Sunshine and Lollipops. He had arranged scholarships for some of those girls who had written the earnest letters in defense of Prom Dreams.

Yesterday, he had rented an apartment for his father. It was just down the block from the garden project that would never become a parking lot. After he had rented the apartment, he had wandered down there, and looked at the flowers and the vegetables growing in cheery defiance of the concrete all around them, and he had known this would be a good place for his father to come to.

Then Houston had seen Mary Bedford working alone, weeding around delicate new spinach tops. He had gone to her, and been humbled by her delight in seeing him. He had told her his father would soon be new to the neighborhood. He had not told her anything that would bring out the drowning kitten kind of sympathy—for his father would hate that—but he had asked her if she could make him welcome here.

His phone rang beside the bed.

"Houston, it's Miss Viv."

"What can I do for you, Miss Viv?" *Please,*

nothing that will test my resolve. Don't ask me to be near her.

"It's about Molly."

He closed his eyes, steeling himself to say no to whatever the request was.

"I have a terrible feeling she's involved herself in an Internet affair. You know how dangerous those can be, don't you?"

"What? Molly? That doesn't sound like Molly." Even though his heart felt as if it was going to pound out of his chest, he forced himself to be calm. "What would make you think that?"

"After I came back from my holiday, Molly just wasn't herself. She didn't seem interested in work. She wouldn't accept the position as head of Second Chances and seemed angry at me, though she wouldn't say why. She lost weight. She had big circles under her eyes. She looked exhausted, as if she may have been crying, privately."

Not an Internet affair, he thought, sick, *a cad.*

"But then, about a week ago, everything changed. She started smiling again. I didn't feel as if she was angry with me. In fact, Houston, she became radiant. Absolutely radiant. I know a woman in love when I see one."

In love? With someone other than him? This new form of torture he had not anticipated.

"Then, just out of the blue, she announced she was going on holidays. I just know she's met someone on the Internet! And fallen in love with them. Houston, she's foolish that way."

I know.

"Did she say she'd met someone?" he asked, amazed by how reasonable he made his voice sound.

"She didn't have to! She said she's done experiencing her dreams through a picture on her living room wall! She said she was going to California for a while."

"What do you want me to do?" he asked.

"I don't know," Miss Viv wailed. "But I need to know she's safe."

That's funny. So did he.

"I'll look after it," he said.

"But how?" This said doubtfully. "California is a big place, Houston!"

He thought of the picture on Molly's living room wall. "It's not that big," he said.

Molly sighed with absolute contentment, and looked over the incredible view. The sun was setting over the Napa Valley. It was as beautiful as she had ever dreamed it could be.

Of course, maybe that was because she was in love.

Finally.

With herself.

Molly sat on a stone patio, high up on a terraced hillside that overlooked the famous vineyards of the Napa Valley in California. The setting sun gilded the grapevines in gold, and the air was as mild as an embrace. She was alone, wearing casual slacks and a T-shirt from a winery she had visited earlier in the day.

She had the feather boa wrapped around her neck.

In front of her was a wineglass of the finest crystal, a precious bottle of Cabernet Sauvignon this Valley was so famous for producing.

For a while after Houston had gone, she had

thought she would die. Literally, Molly had thought she would curl up in a ball in a corner somewhere in her apartment and die.

But she didn't. She couldn't.

Baldy needed her.

And then one day she went to Sunshine and Lollipops to do a routine visit for a report that needed to be filled out for a grant.

All the children, every single one of them, were wearing new shoes.

"An anonymous donor," one of the staff told her. "A whole truckload of them arrived."

Something in Molly had become alert, as if she was reaching for an answer that she couldn't quite grasp.

The next day there had been an excited message on her answering machine.

"Miss Michaels, it's Carmen Sanchez." Tears, Spanish mixed with English, more tears. *"I got a scholarship. I don't know how. I never even applied for one."*

And that feeling of alertness inside Molly had grown. And then, when the second call came, from another one of the girls who had written a letter for Prom Dreams, the alertness sighed within her, *knowing*.

And with that knowing had come a revelation: she had always known the truth about Houston Whitford.

It was her own truth that she had not been so sure of.

Even though he would never admit it, she could clearly see he understood love at a level that she had missed.

It didn't rip down. It didn't tear apart. It didn't wallow in self-pity. It didn't curl up in a corner and die.

Those who had been lucky enough to know it gave back. They danced with life. They embraced *everything:* heartbreak, too. They never stopped believing good could come from bad.

She had told *him* that love could heal all things.

But then she had not lived it. Not believed it. Not ever embraced it as her own truth.

Now she was going to do just that. She was going to be made *better* by the fact, that ever so briefly, she had known the touch and the grace and the glory of loving. She was going to take that and give it to a world that had always waited for her to *see*.

Herself.

So, she watched with a full heart as the light faded over the Napa Valley. She felt as if the radiance within her matched the golden sun.

Headlights were moving up the hill toward the bed and breakfast where she was staying, and she watched them pierce the growing blackness, marveled at how something so simple could be so beautiful, marveled at how a loving heart could *see*.

The car pulled into the parking lot, below her perch, and she watched as a man got out.

In the fading light and at this distance, the man looked amazingly like Houston, that dark shock of hair, the way he carried himself with such masculine confidence, grace.

Of course, who didn't look like Houston? Every dark haired stranger made her heart beat faster. At first, in her curl-up-in-the-corner phase, she had hated that. But as she came to embrace the truth about herself, she didn't anymore.

It was a reminder that she had been given a gift from him. And when she saw someone who reminded her of him now, she allowed herself to tenderly explore what she felt, and send a silent blessing to him.

To love him in a way that was pure because it wished only the best for him and asked for nothing in return.

It wasn't the same as not expecting enough of someone like Chuck, because really getting tangled with someone like Chuck meant you had not expected enough of yourself!

The man disappeared inside the main door far below the patio she sat on, and Molly allowed the beating of her heart to return to normal. She took another sip of wine, watched the vineyards turn to dusky gold as the light faded from the sky.

"Hello."

She turned and looked at him, felt the stillness inside her, the *knowing*. That love was more powerful than he was, than his formidable desire to fight against it.

"Hello," she said softly, back.

"Surprised to see me?"

"Not really," she said.

He frowned at her. "You made yourself damnably hard to find, if you were expecting me."

She smiled.

"Miss Viv was worried that you were having an Internet affair."

"And you? Were you worried about that?"

"Impossible," he whispered.

"Then why did you come?"

He sighed and took the chair across from her. "Because I couldn't *not* come."

They sat there silently for a moment.

"The feathers look good on you," he said after a while.

"Thank you."

"Where's Baldy?"

"I left him with a neighbor."

"Oh."

Again the silence fell. She noticed it was comfortable. *Full,* somehow.

"I owe you an apology," he said.

"No," she said, "you don't. I learned more

from you walking away than I could have ever learned from you staying."

He frowned. "That's not what I was going to apologize for. We both know you're better off without me."

We do?

"No, I wanted to apologize for bringing you to the old neighborhood that night. And then for losing it on that guy, the mugger. For not being able to stop. I might have killed him if you hadn't stopped me."

She chuckled, and he glared at her.

"It's not funny."

"Of course it's funny, Houston. I weigh a hundred and thirteen pounds. And I could have stopped you? Don't be ridiculous. You stopped yourself."

"I'm trying to tell you something important."

"I'm all ears."

"I come from chaos," he said. "And violence. That is my legacy. And I am not visiting them on you."

"Why?" she asked softly.

He glared at her.

"Why are you so afraid to visit your legacy on me?"

"Because I love you, damn it!" The admission was hoarse with held in emotion.

"Ah," she said softly, her whole world filling with a light that put the gold of the Napa Valley sunset to shame. "And you're afraid you would hurt me?"

"Yes."

"You told me you hit a boy in high school once."

"True," he said tautly.

"And then what, fourteen or fifteen years later you hit another person? Who was attacking you?"

"I didn't feel like he was attacking me. I felt as though he was attacking you."

"And so defending me, putting your body between me and that threat, taking care of it, that was a *bad* thing? A pattern?"

"I lost control."

She would have laughed out loud at how ludicrous that assessment of himself was, except she saw what he was doing. He was trying to convince himself to climb back on that horse and ride away from her, back to those lonely places.

The thing was, she wasn't letting him ride off alone. That's all there was to it. Somewhere, somehow, this incredible man had lost a sense of who he really was.

But she saw him so clearly. It was as if she held his truth. And no matter what was in it for her, she was leading him back to it. Because suddenly, she understood that's what love did.

"He had a knife, Houston. He was huge. Don't you think you did what you had to do?"

"Overkill," he said. "Inexcusable."

"I'm not buying it, Houston."

He looked her full in the face.

"You're afraid of loving me."

"Yes," he whispered.

"You're afraid I will let you down, just like every other person who should have loved you has let you down."

"Yes," he admitted.

"You're afraid you will let yourself down.

That love will make you do something crazy that you will regret forever."

"Yes," he said absolutely.

"There is a place," she said ever so softly, "where you do not have to be afraid anymore, Houston. Never again."

He looked at her. His eyes begged for it to be true.

She opened her arms.

And he came into them. She reached up and touched his cheek, with reverence, with the tender welcome of a woman who could see right to her gunslinger's soul. She could feel the strong beat of his good, good heart.

"You are a good man, Houston Whitford. A man with the courage to take every single hard thing life has handed you and rise above it."

He didn't speak, just nestled his head against her breast, and he sighed with the surrender of a man who had found his way down from the high and lonely places.

Over the next few days, they gave themselves over to exploring the glory of the Napa Valley.

They took the wine train. They went for long

walks. They drove for miles exploring the country. They stopped at little tucked away restaurants and vineyards, book shops and antique stores. They whiled away sun-filled afternoons sipping wine, holding hands, looking at each other, letting comfortable silences fall.

They laughed until their sides hurt, they talked until their voices were hoarse.

Molly remembered the day she had first met him, looking at herself in that wedding dress, and yearning for all the things it had made her feel: a longing for love, souls joined, laughter shared, long conversations. Lonely no more.

It was their final morning in California when he told her he had a surprise for her. It was so early in the morning it was still dark when he piled her into the car and drove the mazes of those twisting roads to a field.

Where a hot air balloon was anchored, gorgeous, standing against the muted colors of early morning.

It seemed to pull against its ropes, its brilliant stripes of color—purple, red, green, yellow— straining to join the cobalt-blue of the sky.

She walked toward it, her hand in Houston's, ready for this adventure. Eager to embrace it. She let Houston help her into the basket.

As the pilot unleashed the ropes and they floated upward to join the sky, she leaned back into Houston.

"I have waited all my life for this," Molly whispered.

"For a ride in a hot air balloon?"

"No, Houston," she said softly.

For this feeling—of being whole and alive. In fact, it had nothing to do with the balloon ride and everything to do with love. Over the last few days, it had seeped into her with every breath she took that held Houston's scent.

The hot air heater roared, and the balloon surged upward. The balloon lifted higher as the sun began to rise and drench the vineyards and hillsides in liquid gold. They floated through a pure sky, the world soaked in misty pinks and corals below them.

"Houston, look," she breathed of the view. "It's wonderful. It is better than any dream I ever dreamed."

She glanced at him when he didn't respond. "Is something wrong?"

"I was wondering—" he said, and then he stopped and looked away. He cleared his throat, uncharacteristically awkward.

"What?" she asked, growing concerned.

"Would you like some cheese?"

He produced a basket with an amazing array of cheese, croissants warm from the oven.

"Thank you," she said. "Um, this is good. Aren't you going to have some?"

He was working on uncorking a bottle of wine.

It was way too early for wine. She didn't care. She took a glass from him, sipped it, met his eyes.

"Houston, what is wrong with you?"

"Um, look, I was wondering—" he stopped, took a sudden interest in the scenery. "What's that?" he demanded of the pilot.

The pilot named the winery.

"Are you afraid of heights?" she breathed. This man, nervous, uptight, was not her Houston!

"No, just afraid."

Only a few days ago he wouldn't have admitted fear to her if he'd been dropped into a bear den covered in honey. She eyed him, amazed at his awkwardness. He was now staring at his feet. He glanced up at her.

"I told you," she reminded him gently, "that there is a place where you don't have to be afraid anymore."

"What if I told you I wanted to be in that place, with you, forever?"

His eyes met hers, and suddenly he wasn't fumbling at all.

In a voice as steady as his eyes, he said, "I was wondering if you would consider spending the rest of your life with me."

Her mouth fell open, and tears gathered behind her eyes. "Houston," she breathed.

"Damn. I forgot. Hang on." He let go of her hand, fished through the pocket of the windbreaker he had worn, fell to one knee. He held a ring out to her. The diamonds turned to fire as the rays of the rising sun caught on their facets.

"Molly Michaels, I love you. Desperately. Completely. With every beat of my heart and with every breath that I take. I love you," he said, his voice suddenly his own, strong and sure, a man who had always known exactly what he wanted. "Will you marry me?"

"Yes," she said. Simply. Softly. No one word had ever felt so right in her entire life.

It was yes to him, but also yes to herself. It was *yes* to life, in all its uncertainty. It was *yes* to disappointments being healed, *yes* to taking a chance, *yes* to being fully alive, *yes* to coming awake after sleeping.

And then they were in each other's arms. Houston's lips welcomed her.

Their kiss celebrated, not the miracle of a balloon rising hundreds of feet above the earth, defying gravity, but the absolute miracle of love.

He kissed her again with tenderness that *knew* her. And just like that they were both home.

At long last, after being lost for so long, and alone for so long, they had both found their way home.

EPILOGUE

HOUSTON WHITFORD sat on the bench in Central Park feeling the spring sunshine warm him, his face lifted to it.

The park was quiet.

Peripherally he was aware of Molly and his father coming back down the park path toward him. They had wandered off together to admire the beds of tulips that his father, the gardener, loved so much.

Houston focused on them, his father so changed, becoming more shrunken and frail every day. Molly's arm and his father's were linked, her head bent toward her beloved "Hughie" as she listened to something he was telling her.

Houston saw her smile, saw his father glance at her, the older man's gaze astounded and filled with wonder as if he could not believe how his daughter-in-law had accepted him into her life.

This is what Houston had learned about love: it could not heal all things.

For instance, it could not heal the cancer that ate at his father. It could not heal the fact that he woke from his frequent sleeps with tears of regret sliding down his face.

Love, powerful as it was, could not change the scar left on a nose broken by a father's fury, or the other scars not quite as visible.

No, love could not heal all things.

But it could heal some things. And most days, that was enough. More than enough.

Once, his father had looked at Molly, and said sadly, "That's the woman your mother could have been had I been a better man."

"Maybe," Houston had said gently, feeling that wondrous thing that was called forgiveness. "Or maybe I'm the man you could have been if she had been a better woman."

Now, the baby carriage that Houston had taken charge of while Molly took his father to look at the tulips vibrated beneath where his fingertips rested on the handle, prewail warning. Then his daughter was fully awake, screaming, the carriage rattling as her legs and arms began to flail with fury.

Like her mother in so many ways, he thought with tender amusement, redheaded and bad-tempered.

At the sound of the cry, Houston's father quickened his steps on the path, breaking free of Molly's arm in his hurry to get to the baby.

He arrived, panting alarmingly from the small exertion. He peered at the baby and every hard crease his life and prison had put in his face seemed to melt. He put his finger in the carriage, and the baby latched on to it with her surprisingly strong little fist.

"There, there," his father crooned, "Pappy's here."

The baby went silent, and then cooed, suddenly all charm.

For a suspended moment, it seemed all of them—his father, Molly, the baby, Houston himself—were caught in a radiance of light that was dazzling.

"I lived long enough to see this," his father said, his voice hoarse with astonishment and gratitude, his finger held completely captive by the baby.

"A good thing," Houston said quietly.

"No. More. A miracle," his father, a man who had probably never known the inside of a church, and who had likely shaken his fist at God nearly every waking moment of every day of his life, whispered.

Houston felt Molly settle on the bench beside him, rest her head on his shoulder, nestle into him with the comfort of a woman who knew beyond a shadow of a doubt that she was loved and cherished above all things.

"How's my Woman-of-the-Year?" he asked.

"Oh, stop," she said, but kissed his cheek.

She had taken Second Chances to the next level, beyond what anyone had ever seen for it, or dreamed for it. He liked to think his love helped her juggle so many different roles, all of them with seeming effortlessness, all of them infused with her great joy and enthusiasm for life.

Houston put his arm around her, pulled her in closer to him, touched his lips to her forehead.

His father was watching him, his eyes went back to Molly and then rested on Houston, satisfied, content, *full*.

"A miracle," he said again.

"Yes, it is," Houston, a man who had once doubted miracles, agreed.

All of it. Life. Love. The power of forgiveness. A place to call home. All of it was a miracle, so sacred a man could not even contemplate it without his heart nearly bursting inside his chest.

"Yes," he repeated quietly. "It is."